The Shame

The Shame

a novel

MAKENNA GOODMAN

MILKWEED EDITIONS

The characters and events in this book are fictitious. Any similarity to real persons, living or dead, is coincidental and not intended by the author.

Published 2020 by Milkweed Editions
Printed in Canada
Cover art direction by Mary Austin Speaker
Cover artwork and lettering by Leanne Shapton
20 21 22 23 24   5 4 3 2 1
First Edition

Milkweed Editions, an independent nonprofit publisher, gratefully acknowledges sustaining support from the Alan B. Slifka Foundation and its president, Riva Ariella Ritvo-Slifka; the Ballard Spahr Foundation; *Copper Nickel*; the McKnight Foundation; the National Endowment for the Arts; the National Poetry Series; the Target Foundation; and other generous contributions from foundations, corporations, and individuals. Also, this activity is made possible by the voters of Minnesota through a Minnesota State Arts Board Operating Support grant, thanks to a legislative appropriation from the arts and cultural heritage fund. For a full listing of Milkweed Editions supporters, please visit milkweed.org.

Library of Congress Cataloging-in-Publication Data

Names: Goodman, Makenna, author.
Title: The shame : a novel / Makenna Goodman.
Description: First edition. | Minneapolis, Minnesota : Milkweed Editions, 2020. | Summary: "The Shame is a novel about technology, capitalism, motherhood, and the search for meaningful art"-- Provided by publisher.
Identifiers: LCCN 2019057345 (print) | LCCN 2019057346 (ebook) | ISBN 9781571311368 (trade paperback) | ISBN 9781571317230 (ebook)
Classification: LCC PS3607.O585 S53 2020 (print) | LCC PS3607.O585 (ebook) | DDC 813/.6--dc23
LC record available at https://lccn.loc.gov/2019057345
LC ebook record available at https://lccn.loc.gov/2019057346

Milkweed Editions is committed to ecological stewardship. We strive to align our book production practices with this principle, and to reduce the impact of our operations in the environment. We are a member of the Green Press Initiative, a nonprofit coalition of publishers, manufacturers, and authors working to protect the world's endangered forests and conserve natural resources. *The Shame* was printed on acid-free 100% postconsumer-waste paper by Friesens Corporation.

For Sam

The Shame

One

Imagine you're in the middle of the state of Vermont, on a tiny island the size of a shoebox. Around you is a lake of boiling lava, so hot that it burns up anything it touches. In one hand you have an endlessly replenishing supply of undercooked egg whites and a straw. This will keep you alive for a long and unhappy life. At the edge of the lava, miles and miles away, the heat ends and there is a lush and beautiful forest, meadows with wildflowers, bubbling brooks with salmon and little icicles and wild mint. There you can eat whatever you want. There you can eat pasta with clams, pasta with cheese, pasta with toppings unlike anything you could imagine—and there are salads with every possible ingredient and really good dressing—all of which will be available for the rest of your long and happy life. But to get to this magical place you have to cross the hot lava, and you can't have a flying machine. Would you do it? How would you do it?

Here's how I would do it. I'd take my gun, because you didn't say I couldn't have one. I'd take my gun and I would look up in the sky and I would see a giant flock of migrating geese. I'd put my egg whites down on the shoebox island and aim my gun and shoot a goose, which would fall down into the lava beside me. Because of the size of the goose, only the bottom half would burn instantly, and I'd have two seconds to use the top half as a stepping-stone. By this time I would have already shot down a second goose. As one foot lifted off the first bird, the other foot would be landing on the second, and by then I'd have shot down a third. I'd be in a spree of shooting geese one by one, rapid-fire, and dead geese would be raining down on me, dropping into the lava in a line, and I'd be hopping from one to the next while shooting down more, and this would go on for hours and hours—until, finally, I would have shot down the very last goose, which would take me to the edge of the hot lava, and I would jump safely onto the shore of the bountiful pasta and salad forest, and live happily ever after.

———

There are few moments in our lives when we are truly nowhere. I had experienced this feeling only a few times: Once, on top of a mountain that I had scaled just after dawn. Again, at an indexing conference; the hotel I stayed at was filled with all shades of corporate people convening, and I spent what turned out to be a great night watching pay-per-view and ordering lasagna to my room. And now, as I drove through darkness on the interstate.

I messed with the dial until I got to public radio jazz, which, aside from my thoughts, was my only company. As I drove, I began to notice a sensation in my body that was unmistakably good, even euphoric. I was free. Behind me in the back seat were two empty car seats. No one was asking me for a snack, no one's nose needed to be wiped, no one demanded the same song be played at top volume over and over. I turned my music up and drank some water. I never went anywhere without my water bottle, and there was always a full one in my car. I never got my hair cut either. The hairstylist always does shit you don't ask for, and you leave looking like a senator's wife. I do the two-hack snip after the shower, and I always look fine.

I put my water bottle down onto cough drop wrappers in the cup holder and saw a half-sucked one stuck to the console. Next to it was a crust of stale bread and some broken baby sunglasses, like bird skeletons. My engine light was on. What was I doing? This was too extreme. At the next exit, I told myself, I would turn back. I could get home while the kids were still asleep. Asa would be amazed I had gone as far as I did. Maybe that distance was enough. But the portion of interstate I was on had very few exits, and I was low on gas. I kept driving until I reached the next rest area and pulled in to fill up the tank. It was cold. Mine was the only car at the pumps. I went in to use the bathroom and met no one. By the time I got back into my car, I had made my decision.

———

How did I get here? Who registered my car? Who scrambled my eggs, took me to the dentist, made corn on the cob, refrigerated the butter? I dive into the pond but emerge the same person. I push around the shopping cart, and another woman's hands grab the granola. I am Asa's wife. I want to go to a party, he doesn't. So I stay home. I want to go to a town meeting, he doesn't; I go but then come up with an excuse to leave early and drive home fast on icy roads. He turns over in bed snoring the second the light goes out, I lie there staring at the dark air above my head. He went on a fishing trip with Phin and came back, was all over me, oh how he missed me. I wanted to stay up and watch Netflix and eat popcorn in bed. Maybe if I lived in Paris. Maybe if I were fifty-two, had a miniature poodle, were a famous painter with a yellow sports car and a rubber plant in a giant pot and a coffee table covered with elaborate silver teaware. Not in this life, Asa says. You married the wrong person. Oh, but what the fuck does he know, with his elbow patches? I can reupholster the couch, I can adopt a puppy, I can wear whatever I want, do whatever I want to do with whomever I want to do it with. Maybe if I wrote a successful novel, I would go to Paris to celebrate, dance on tables and smoke a pipe. Maybe if I hadn't skipped history class in high school to smoke cigarettes in the alley, I would have a doctorate in international relations and would live in Paris for my job. Maybe if I had stuck with my singing in middle school, I'd be in a conservatory and would go to Paris each month to perform. I would stay in a rented flat, I would know the landlord. I would buy groceries and carry them in a woven bag.

———

I was stalked by an ex-boyfriend in college. He would show up at my window at four in the morning and throw pebbles, demanding that I see him. I told him calmly, and then more forcefully, to go away, and a week later a shoebox arrived on my front doorstep. Inside was a dead squirrel. This seemed like the last straw, like I would be the next to go. Wasn't that the message he was trying to send? I took the shoebox to the college counselor to file a complaint, along with my best friend, who was also my housemate. The administration building was low, made of cement like a storage unit. The counselor asked me if perhaps this was his attempt at romance. Maybe it was misguided, she conceded, fine. She recalled her childhood in Kansas, where boys used to climb up a tree and knock on her bedroom window, where kids would beat each other with sticks on the playground and then go home for cookies and milk. I told her another story, about a time when the same guy came into my living room with a gun, pointing it at his head and then mine, alternating. (My friend shifted in her chair; the story wasn't true.) The counselor paused, then, tucking a tissue she was holding into her shirtsleeve, told me they'd park a public safety vehicle outside my house for two days. In the meantime, I should think seriously about taking a leave of absence: go home as soon as possible, she said, pack my bags today, wait until the guy graduated, then come back and finish up my classes, take my finals, write my thesis. This was the plan she had for me, and she started closing her folder as if to say, "Time's up." I walked out of there and decided just to leave it all up to fate. Life went on as usual; the 4:00 a.m. visits subsided and he shacked up with a field hockey player. Latest news is he's representing women in domestic abuse cases. I guess I got lucky. But the way she tucked that wet tissue into her sleeve really stuck with me. I kept wondering if it was just a thing people did, old people, to save paper. Or maybe she didn't have pockets.

A few years later I was living in Madrid, interning at a film company for the summer and renting a room in a colorfully painted apartment in Chueca with other foreigners. The landlord came up to talk once a week, shirtless, jiggling, and we'd share slices of the peaches I bought compulsively at the fruit stand downstairs. I slept in the pink room. It had a high ceiling. I could hear the discotecas bumping, but I went to bed early. That year was the hottest summer on record, and you could walk only on the shady side of the street. No one went outside from noon to two. I slept with the fan on high five inches from my face, and one morning I woke up and couldn't move my neck. My employer recommended a massage parlor down the street from our office, and the next day, after doing a piss-poor job of translating the film company's website copy, I went in for an appointment. The massage therapist was a man with long hair. There was Muzak and lavender. After the back massage I flipped over, and he ventured down to my groin. He inserted his fingers in me, pressed them against my pubic bone from inside, explained to me in broken English something about pressure points. He proceeded cautiously, waiting to see if I approved. I told him I was getting a migraine and went back to the office, where I said nothing. We had bocadillos for lunch, gazpacho. I spent the rest of the summer in solitude, walking instead of taking the metro because there had been a bombing. I sometimes visited the vintage store across the street from my apartment; the manager was fun-loving and we would laugh about bullshit. I read English gossip magazines. I was lonely. I didn't want to get blown up, it was so hot, and I had the ache in my neck that wouldn't go away. Why didn't I tell anyone? Oh, please.

It wasn't just the bombing. Ever since I was little, I've been terrified by the idea of untimely death. Having children only made it worse. Waves of fear will wash over me while I'm scrubbing the dishes or driving my children around for a nap, or when they have fevers and I'm next to them in bed with a cool cloth, counting their inhalations. I imagine my kids bent over, shoulders shaking while they weep, calling for their mother, "Mama," and their father unable to find the right words to soothe them. I imagine them cold and alone in their beds, crying out in the night for me, and me not being able to wrap them in my arms, to tell them it will be okay, to comfort them. I will be dead. Forever. I have written "put together a will" on my to-do list every week, but I never actually do it. I worry that once I have my affairs in order, I will drop dead right then and there.

The thing that frightens me most, maybe, is the idea that Asa (or, if he dies first, my kids) won't know what to do with my body. I imagine what they will say: "Bury her in the local cemetery, so we have somewhere to visit." But then I think of the work involved: the beating back of the weeds with pesticides so the grass looks like a golf course; the interminable mowing; and then the space the dead take up when there are living people who need room for shelter; and the chemicals pumped into hollowed-out bodies that lie like mummies in tombs; the deterioration, slowly fleshing off to bone while the toxic death makeup leaches into the groundwater; and the skeletons that are there for all eternity, gaping, with their clothes still on, their braids still growing!

"Cremate her," they might suggest, and that option is also no good—how would they know the ashes were mine? "Compost her," Asa's more radical peers could say. "Inoculate her with spores." But wearing a mushroom suit in a hole in the ground? Perhaps I'm too vain.

As I drove, I imagined the scene of my memorial, and

what began as terror morphed into a state of enjoyment and relaxation, so that I began tapping my hands on the steering wheel to the future rhythm of beating drums and kids playing tambourines. My shoulders dropped a little. I let myself release into it. I turned up the music, letting it swell along with my reverie as I drove.

Here's how it will go: Asa will invite my community to a weekend camping trip in the mountains. Everyone will drive there, having time to think in the car, passing small towns and meadows full of wildflowers, listening to songs from the past on the radio. They will arrive at a suitable site, near a stream, and set up camp, and they will bring me over to the creek and wash my body with cold water. They will try not to slip, but they'll inevitably get wet. Then they'll dab my skin with rosewater and or-ganic oils and place a bundle of lavender in my hands, tied with simple twine. They will wrap me, naked, in a white linen sheet, and carry me back to the campsite on a cliff with a view of mountains. There will be a pile of wood prepared for a bonfire. They will place me on top of the pile—I guess using a ladder—and the music will begin. Everyone who wants to will play an instrument, in a circle surrounding me, and there will be singing. My friends are talented; this will be a memorable display of their artistry. There will be maracas, shakers, fiddles, whatever they feel like playing. There will be children dancing. Maybe my children, maybe my grandchildren. There will be songs I loved, old folk songs, old blues songs. The fire will be lit. Asa—or, if he's dead, too, whoever is in charge—will make sure it burns bright, even if it means adding some sort of gas. (Me being partially burned is not an option.) And then, as the flames rage, the music will die down, and there will be a picnic where people can share memories or stories as they please. There will be good wine and beer, a potluck. Someone will remember to bring the chips and that store-bought onion dip I always hovered around apologetically at children's birthday parties. People will have the option of weeping into their salad, but grief won't be a requirement. The idea is, celebrate. Then, after I'm all up in smoke, the campers will pack their things and leave me there, hovering like a low cloud cover, as they depart to a bed-and-breakfast or a distant campsite with clean air. If the memorial starts in the morning, I want them gone by dusk. No sleeping out there in the dark. I'll be dead, but they'll be alive.

I found myself looking forward to this moment, some small part of me, even though I fear death utterly. Just knowing I can control it, through planning the details, calms me. I want my kids, for years to come, to remember the celebration, the burning, the feast, the music, the washing of my body in the cold water. I want them to be able to go back to the site year after year if they feel like it, to collide with nature, not a fixed and frigid tombstone, and to come to terms with the fact that I am dead, that they will lose others, that they, too, will die and so will their kids. If their response is to resent me, then so be it.

But eventually, they'll thank me.

If the day of my death is soon, there is a letter that I want someone—maybe Asa—to give to my kids. I have left this in a file marked "Important," and it goes like this:

You two,

I'm writing you this letter in the event of my untimely death. I want you, when faced with sorrow and the inevitable yearning to hear my voice, to be able to read my words, meant for you and only you. Can you remember my voice? I want you to know how hard it was, to leave this world, to know—whether on a conscious level or not—that I would never get to hold you again, smell your breath, cut your eggs up, pour you milky tea, caress your softness.

My great fear, which has kept me up nights for years, is that you will have to live without a mother when you need one the most. And now, perhaps, that fear has been realized. But your lives have to go on. There are still peanut butter sandwiches to eat, even if I'm not making them; they're just sandwiches. You can still feed the crusts to the dog. Someone will fill your water bottles, brush your teeth with you. There will be someone to make sure you are taken care of. But what will you do when the grief becomes impossible to bear?

Your father: he knew me best. He took the broom and dustpan to my corners. Just ask him—anything—about me. He'll tell you the story of the day we spent at North Beach, shrieking in the water, chasing your kickboards, eating twist soft serve at a picnic table, watching the bodies of Canadian tourists. He'll tell you he couldn't even look at them, how no one could compare; he'll give a grandfatherly wink. He'll tell you how we biked as the mountains cut out of the water, how Phin went five miles without stopping at age four, no training wheels. Or he'll tell you about the drive to the birthing center, me on hands and knees in the back of the Subaru with one seat folded down and rain falling in sheets as he drove seventy-five miles an hour on winding country lanes, how the pimply nighttime guard at the emergency room entrance couldn't find the right key, how I held my legs together until he did, how we somehow made it around the corner to the hospital bed. He'll tell you how we ordered breakfast sandwiches and seltzer from the birthing center café and watched professional soccer on the world's smallest television, while I waddled to and from the bathroom peeing blood, calling for more ice diapers. Cuddling Eden in my arms like a seal pup.

I worked hard to love you, to make you feel loved, to have the world love you. I became old instantly. I became imprisoned by love, by impatience, by impetuousness. It wasn't easy; I hope you will find the shadows comforting, in the end. I wish I could be there to defend myself.

Love,
Your mother

I change it about once a week.

Just over a year ago Asa was offered tenure, and there was a dinner in his honor. The president of the college and his wife had reserved the entirety of a restaurant twenty minutes from our house, run by a couple who had recently moved to Vermont from Boston and had teamed up with a renowned chef. The chairs of other departments were invited, as well as some deans and upper administrative staff. At the time I peppered my husband with questions: Who were their wives, what did they do, how many children did they have, did they send their kids to private school, had he seen the women before, were they intelligent?

I hadn't worked, officially, since the summer before Phin was born. About two years before that, I had written a short novel about an eccentric French stepmother, but it never found a publisher. My mother had always wanted me to be a successful writer, as she herself wanted to be, and I tried to publish it, I think, as an obligatory gesture to her memory, or at least I told this to myself. But no one liked it, and no one offered me a deal, and so I shifted my focus to getting pregnant, having babies, and performing relatively insignificant and infrequent freelance indexing jobs (which I wasn't that good at, truth be told), a useful skill left over from my college days when I badly needed cash. These indexes, mostly for medical textbooks, offered no creative satisfaction; I didn't even really like seeing words pile up, or their corresponding numbers. (I hated doing my taxes.) I would get lost in thought and have to redo my work often. But the indexes brought in a modicum of money, and that was enough. On the door to my studio was a bumper sticker that read: "If you don't talk to your kids about indexing, who will?"

I began painting on the side, something I had watched my father doing while I was growing up, and I used it as a meditation since I never really had much time to make sincere work with all the other chores required on a homestead. I did a series of my grandmother's teacups that I hung on a wall of the kitchen, and a portrait of the painter Vanessa Bell lying faceup in water, which I hung in the mudroom. They were a little bit Bloomsbury Group, a little bit paint-by-number. I was okay with that. It was affirming to have created something material I could walk by and actually look at or take down, dust off, hold in my hands.

When I was on deadline, I worked while the kids were at school; otherwise, I cleaned the house, even though it was never clean enough. On the weekends I took both kids for walks in the double stroller up the steep dirt road, turning around at the top and bracing backward, my weight the only thing keeping them from barreling down the road or off into a drainage ditch. The money I made on the rare index didn't add much to our family's bottom line, but it allowed me to feel that I was contributing in the most minor sense. The household items I purchased online, for example, felt paid for by the sweat of my brow, and somehow this made my increasingly conventional marriage feel more balanced.

Although I tidied, our home was always messy, but as a whole it retained an energy that was aesthetically intoxicating. Besides cleaning, cooking, rearranging the art and furniture, and doing the laundry, I trolled eBay on our spotty wireless for bargains to make everything beautiful. Vintage velvet pillowcases for the couch, a universal slipcover for a shabby antique wingback chair we had inherited from a neighbor (which took me nearly half a day to find online and probably wasn't worth it, in the end, as it was too loose in places and impossible to iron), discounted duvet covers for our bed, and a yellow spatula that could actually reach around the blade at the bottom of the blender. We were also lucky enough to be the recipients of quality hand-me-downs, and the objects around me comforted me; they had a legacy. I considered myself frugal for researching pre-owned items carefully and finding the cheapest deal for the best quality, though ideologically all the online purchasing made me wonder if I was a chief contributor to the over-consumptive economy we had traveled so far to escape in the first place. But, as rural people living on the edges of a Vermont village that didn't even have a gas station, would we do better to get in the car and drive forty-five minutes to a drugstore chain only to risk not finding the thing we were looking for? Sure, there was a local feedstore for things like chicken grain and what we called "government cheese," a thirteen-dollar shrink-wrapped hunk of sharp cheddar, but that was about it. Asa and I accepted the paradoxes of small-town life in the modern world while still considering ourselves renegades and anti-capitalist at the core.

My attempts at frugality didn't prevent the occasional argument with Asa, who, despite his salary as a college professor (not that big, considering), wore old socks and T-shirts he would discover after digging through duffel bags in the attic, handed down to him nearly a decade earlier by his older brother. I braced myself for his commentary on purchases he deemed superfluous or, worse, frivolous: blueberries in winter, almond instead of peanut butter, a bigger terra-cotta pot for the aloe plant. Fine, I had a bit of a fetish for brightly colored water bottles, kids' Tupperware, and handwoven African baskets, but otherwise I was pretty conservative with my spending. I knew I should resist the impulse to buy these excessive containers destined to take up valuable space in our lives, but it still got old, always having to explain the receipt, item by item, after returning home from the grocery store.

This is what really bothered me, when I was honest with myself—I was a failure in the world of art. I was afraid I had become the very thing I feared: my mother, who had struggled to make it as a writer and ultimately didn't, and who died imagining two little men were always following her, living under her eaves, stealing things from her, leaving the seat up, hiding cheese rinds under the daybed, making creases in the sheets, and hoarding newspapers. She tried her whole life, hired a nanny to raise me, even got a few minor book deals, but in the end still had nothing in her bank account except the dwindling reserves of investments she had made from selling my father's paintings after he died.

I was also worried about being left. I imagined the day would finally arrive when Asa would sit me down to explain why he had fallen out of love with me, and how he was moving into a yurt with his new (younger) girlfriend and would take the kids to live with them, and she would wear see-through nightgowns all the time, and it wasn't my fault, but blah blah blah. I woke up in night sweats each time I had this dream, in different variations, over and over again: him leaving me, my devastation, raging, then breaking down. Sometimes in the dreams I would receive emails from people telling me that my marriage was a waste. I would shake Asa awake, asking him to promise never to cheat, begging him to admit he was. He would roll over and tell me to stop wasting my energy on obsessive fantasy. But I needed his affirmation. Without it, I was sure I would disappear. Yes, I felt invisible. I didn't have anything to show for myself except my kids, and the older they got, the more themselves they became, while I grew more and more servile, adhering always to their changing needs. As a result, I was anxious about the dinner with the president of the college. I was worried I'd have nothing to say.

For three weeks before the dinner, I did my best to bring my intellect back to life and furiously researched the news from the last several months. If I didn't have something personal to discuss over dinner—for who would want to hear about all the things I really did; a good Yankee didn't divulge such private and insignificant matters—I would be able to discuss current events if it killed me trying. I imagined revealing my daily rituals; I imagined all the other wives raising their eyebrows and asking why I didn't just get a babysitter. What was I going to say, that I was totally attached to my children, and didn't trust anyone to care for them better than I could, perhaps pathologically so? That I didn't want to become my mother, who claimed to have breastfed me but ultimately did little else to contribute to my rearing? That I wasn't even in touch with my nanny, who actually raised me, while someone else raised her daughter, though surely her comforting voice would have gotten me through a time or two? That I wanted my children to have a mother who was at least there, making snacks, carting them to the science museum and the pizza place, who had chosen them over her own ego, her own ambition? Who rubbed their backs when they asked instead of forcing them to put themselves to bed? That cleaning my own house was a question of honor, and also of occupying an otherwise idle mind? No, better to be able to talk about the wider world to show that I could cook, clean, care for my children, support my husband's career, and contribute to the intellectualizing he was being celebrated for. I would look good doing it too.

I thought about this last part a great deal. In those weeks leading up to the dinner, I lay awake each night next to my kids as they fell asleep and went over my outfit in my mind, perfecting it: brown velvet slim-leg pants, a handwoven linen shirt, earrings that were rose petals cast in silver, and gray socks under ankle boots. I finished reading the novel that had been gathering dust on my bedside table. I scrolled through magazine back issues that had been piling up on the shelf in the bathroom. I listened carefully to public radio while driving to and from the co-op so as not to miss the news. It surprised me that I got any joy from what felt like studying for my college finals, especially since I was still trying to please the same type of higher-ups. But I liked the preparation. It felt purposeful. I pushed myself.

Hopefully Asa hadn't mentioned my secret and shameful artistic aspirations to his colleagues; I was grateful he was a man of few words when it came to the personal, although in arguments that was the first thing I raged about. If anyone brought it up, I would deny that I had ever been a writer—and, anyway, I was sure that I had never really been one to begin with. Instead I would say, impressively, "I've taken up painting."

The night arrived. We showered. We dressed. I fastened my earrings, applied some tinted lip balm, took a last look in the mirror, and kissed the kids goodbye. They were already in their pajamas and climbing all over the babysitter, the daughter of a neighbor, whom I didn't trust. This was the first time in over a year that Asa and I had been out together, and I hoped it would be worth it. We sat in silence to begin with, and it occurred to me that he was nervous too. At a certain point I had Asa quiz me on the names of his colleagues as we drove on dirt roads through the hills.

There were name tags at the table. I was seated directly to the right of the president of the college. Now I knew I had been rehearsing for a real reason, likely cosmic. And thanks to my research, I could impress. I could use what I had learned. I could even flirt a little, as I had noticed the president was quite attractive, despite his age. I knew that if I bungled this, Asa would look like a man who had married beneath him, and even though it wouldn't affect his tenure, it would absolutely cement in the president's mind an opinion of me for the rest of Asa's career at the college, which—we hoped—was for a long time if not forever. Ivy League wasn't easy to find in the backwoods; once you got it, you made sure to keep it.

The other wives were put together in just the right way, and in particular the wife of the dean of English. She was tan from a recent trip to some island she and her husband visited every winter, which sounded like a heaven I could never hope to see (five-star hotel, lunch delivered poolside), and had impeccable taste in clothing (loose, relaxed, chic, black). Thankfully, after a glass of wine, I relaxed enough to release her hold on me, to let my childish insecurities fade into the background and allow my adult self to predominate. I was smart, damn it. I was sexy!

Partway through the dinner, right after the fried oyster mushrooms and ramp aioli and just before the salad, I looked around the table to find that many eyes were on

me, as I held the room with my opinions about the war
on drugs, gun control, and the recent death of a musician
I had revered since I was little, who challenged gender
norms and changed the course of music forever. Asa looked
happy. He was smiling and seemed at ease. He fit right in
with the deans but was perhaps more professorial, more
rumpled. We were the bohemians amid the preppies. We
didn't use the dryer; maybe that was it. Whatever it was,
I was hitting all the high notes and barely even trying. I
had an internal script prepared I hadn't even touched on
yet. My husband squeezed my thigh under the table, and I
could see from the corner of my eye how proud he was of
me, how well the night was going, how beautiful I looked.
He was lucky to be able to be both a present father while
also propelling himself in his career, to have his work in
academia buttressed by his life close to the land and for
the establishment to recognize that. He was surrounded by
smart, talented, powerful thinkers and yet could disappear
daily into his hand-built farmhouse to make homemade
soup on the Bauhaus-inspired two-burner stove, tend the
garden, build a stone wall, design and construct a movable
outdoor pizza oven, putter in the woodshop, cross-country
ski out the doorstep into the woods, and forage for wild
edibles. He had it all. And a captivating wife! What a team
we were.

Yes, I was winning them all over. Our discussion was
the perfect combination of agreeability and combative-
ness. The salad came and went. I challenged conservative

assertions in just the right tone and could see I made some of the wives stop and think, when discussing the merits of public versus private education. What was a better choice, "blessing" the under-resourced public school with your presence and thinking that was enough to address the problems of segregation, or creating a radical, inexpensive, nondogmatic private school to show the public sector their model wasn't working and give them an example of one that might? We spoke of hunting and the politics of ecological agriculture, and I went on for some time about nutrient density and the difference between merely "organic" food and that which is deeply nourishing on a micronutrient level. There is a big difference; a carrot is not just a carrot. At my suggestion we even played the "Which dessert are you?" personality game, my favorite—a gamble, to be sure, but it went over really well. Everyone was so relaxed; I was a breath of fresh air to them, you could tell.

I wasn't faking this, mind you. Yes, I'd had to read some back issues, but they had always been around. I was the one who had subscribed to them in the first place. A lot of this was, in fact, my area of interest. And while I might not have had success in the world of the written word, I wasn't a pudding (though in the dessert game, of course, I was). This was an important exercise for me, knowing that I still had a brain; I still had something to give. I began to feel as if I, too, had been offered the promotion. Asa's boss, the president (chocolate person; very picky!), laughed with me about something, elbowing me in the arm as if we had known each other since the good old days, and the wife of the chair of the medieval studies department invited me to a private meditation group at her guesthouse on Sunday mornings. She was a classic pie person, and we found out all about her top-secret recipe for the flakiest crust (something pie people always do, try to convert you). I had another glass of wine. The conversation kept flowing. I could have stayed all night. Everyone was focused on me, amazed at how much I knew, considering I wasn't a "professional" woman, how I was the only stay-at-home mom at the table who didn't hire someone to clean her house, who gardened, who raised sheep, who dabbled in freelance work, who was an artist, who knew that painting is not just drawing with paint but the placement of color next to color, who had time to read long-form journalism while taking care of two kids and making dinner every night, sewing patches on pants instead of buying new pairs. I could see a glimmer of envy in the other wives' faces when I discussed the projects and nature hikes I organized for my kids, the forts we'd built, that they used real knives to cut real vegetables. Yes, eyes were on me. And my audience was speechless, it seemed, as I digressed and divulged exactly how to make sauerkraut; it's all about process, but it's actually quite simple!

After a while I discovered that, yes, while all eyes were on me, the interest and admiration in the other wives' eyes didn't seem right, exactly. Could it be that it was closer to horror? What had I said, oh *shit*, had I said something wrong, had I joked about homeschoolers in a pejorative way, not knowing that someone's cousins were unschooling their kids on a nearby farm? I hadn't brought up vaccinations or astrology, oh god, had I? And then the head of admissions, who was sitting directly across from me, stifled a laugh, and as he covered his mouth, his wife (cake person, sugar fiend) slapped him on the shoulder. I took a breath and reached for my water glass to buy some time, to slow down and regroup. But my hands, I found, were occupied. Distracted by my own pontificating, I had been—for who knows how long, but clearly long enough—cutting the president's filet mignon, and when I looked down at his plate, I could see that I had done a very good job indeed; the pieces were spaced evenly apart and in neatly arranged cubes, just large enough to spear with a fork, but not too big to choke on.

<hr />

I thought about this now, in my car. What a fool I was, to have expected the feeling of true belonging to be granted to me just because I wanted it badly. These were intellectuals who belonged in that world. They had paid their dues. They were part of the inner circle. There was very little room left. Their wives had been going to those dinners for years, eating the same fried mushrooms again and again as the cycle of new tenured stock repeated itself. At the dinner I had been convinced the women were not serious, but now I realized that was likely an unfair assessment; some were probably doctors on call and couldn't even come to the dinner. And weren't some of the women I'd assumed were wives actually professors themselves? It was embarrassing to me now how predictable I was, how small-minded. I remembered how I had wanted the president to picture me naked while he explained how his poodle, his beloved pet, would give him a full-body hug when he walked into his house. I noticed the sticker on the upper left corner of my windshield; my oil change was long overdue. I thought I had it all figured out, didn't I? Well, look at me now.

———

I keep looping around to the same feeling: fear, in general, about being an adult. The weight of motherhood is a backpack full of stones. Like soil, like a bomb. It's the kind of feeling that grips me like I'm in a foggy valley early in the morning surrounded by thick white air, unable to see even my hand in front of my face, and I don't realize that, a hundred feet up, the sun is out. I have no way of knowing. "Cherish it," a woman told me at the market, smiling at the kids. I wanted to punch her in the fucking face.

I go over the details again and again of the things I've done wrong, and when I'm hovering over them like a drone, replaying the moments where I tripped up, where I failed, I start to feel better. Because I'm important. It's me, after all, who keeps the trains running on time. It's me who makes dinner, who is in charge of no one drowning in the bath, who washes up, scrubs dried egg off the edges of the table, scoops dead flies from the corners of the windowsill with the sponge.

Sometimes, though, I wonder if my children really love me. I think, from a place that feels rational, that they just *need* me. Then I think that maybe it isn't even need at all but an addiction. That if they ran out of their supply of me, they'd have symptoms of withdrawal, but then the need would vanish. Or the need would come back, but it could be satiated by something, or someone, else.

Yes, it's just addiction. They don't even know me. Their knowledge of me is simply how they can get from me what they need. That is my character: a surface to reflect my children's desires, to indicate what trick they need to pull out of their hats to relieve the itch that only I can scratch.

———

I remember, as a small child, seeing my mother yell at my two older sisters and chase them around the kitchen with the silverware container from the dishwasher. Eventually, she discovered that for years she had been living with a tumor pressing down on her right eye, and so we accepted that there were legitimate underpinnings to her rage. She kept smoking anyway, and would sneak down to the basement to do it. She would crack a window and press her lips up to the sash. When I was thirteen, she got the mass removed, and her anger disappeared. But there was more loss; a whole lifetime of the tumor's rage had shaped me.

What would I do with a mother who wasn't vindictive? Who didn't tell me things like, "Now I know why you don't have any friends," or, "Of course he would stop calling you, if you talk to him the way you talk to me." I didn't know what to do with this new mother—the one who was open, who was warm, who was game for anything—so despite her remission, I hated her anyway. I figured the tumor had been her fault all along. She had made it, hadn't she? Why did she get absolution simply because they cut it out? I was the one with my childhood riding piggyback. But now that I'm a mother, I think absolution is more than fair.

⁓

My engine light went off, and I was filled with a sense of relief. I was in Westchester, New York. It was 5:00 a.m. and my adrenaline was wearing off. I stopped at a twenty-four-hour Dunkin' Donuts, drank a cup of coffee, and ate a chocolate donut, things I never do. In an hour, Asa would be giving the kids breakfast. He would drive them to school.

Back in the car, I listened to the news. I put the window down. There was a rush of cold. The darkness had been consuming, but it was nearing light. I became frightened. I worried about my children. I had the urge again to call and make sure they were okay. Life felt suddenly very short, and I felt far away. Why had I been driving blindly to New York like some madwoman? What was I doing, what was I looking for? But of course I knew.

Two

There once was a little boy who lived on a farm. Every morning he woke up, ate an egg-in-a-hole made with eggs from his own chickens, and watched his mother brew coffee in her faded nightshirt. Sometimes, after his father emerged from the bathroom holding the newspaper, the little boy would watch him slip a hand up her shirt as his mother peeped with surprise, like a stuck chick. After breakfast, the little boy would go and visit the laying hens, as it was his job to collect their eggs and give them food and water. The king of the flock was named Mr. Flash, and as the only rooster, he felt very important and protective of his hens. Every morning, Mr. Flash would fluff his tail feathers, crow at the top of his lungs, and—usually while the boy wasn't watching but occasionally when he was—fuck a layer, even though she squirmed to get away, just like nature intended.

The boy wasn't necessarily fond of Mr. Flash, but the rooster provided entertainment and a musicality that set the mood, except when the little boy's sister was napping outside, and his mother shouted, "Goddamnit!" and raced to check underneath the blanket she'd thrown over the stroller to keep her little parrot from waking up and talking. Mr. Flash, despite his regular vulgarity with the hens, did his due diligence keeping order, and on a few occasions he even successfully fought off the neighborhood fox, coming to try his luck at a free lunch. So the little boy's family accepted the fowl's patriarchal benevolence and continued to provide him with food, water, bedding, and all the other demands of a responsible animal husband.

Then, one day, Mr. Flash woke the little boy and his family early with a god-awful crowing, louder than ever before and incessant, as if to announce a change of heart. For Mr. Flash began to show aggressive behavior toward his benefactors, even daring to attack the little boy while he was filling the feed dish and collecting the morning eggs. This was, of course, frightening, though at first the little boy gave the rooster the benefit of the doubt. He would approach Mr. Flash diplomatically with ripe rosehips, only to be lunged at and chased until the boy hurdled over the coop's perimeter fence. Finally the little boy abandoned the treats and resorted to wielding a pine branch as a shield every morning, waving it around desperately to protect himself from Mr. Flash's daggerlike spurs. After nearly a week, the little boy divulged the violence of his mornings to his mother, who was disturbed and who recounted the story to the little boy's father that evening when he returned home from work. And so later that night, while the little boy was sleeping, his father went out with a .22 and killed Mr. Flash, throwing his body into the woods.

The next morning the little boy woke up as usual, came downstairs, and watched his mother make his egg-in-a-hole in her faded nightshirt. He saw his father pour his mother a cup of coffee and give her a loving pat. And then he noticed something different: the rooster hadn't crowed. And when he went outside after breakfast, pine shield in hand, Mr. Flash was nowhere to be seen. The little boy thought this was weird and went inside to tell his father, who was reading the newspaper at the breakfast table, toast hanging from his mouth. His parents followed the little boy to the coop, and agreed that Mr. Flash was missing.

"That's odd," said his father.

"That's strange," said his mother. "Maybe the fox got him."

The fox. Of course! The little boy was sure it was the fox. In fact, he had heard a scuffle outside the night before, as he was falling asleep. That devil. He had finally gotten what he had been wanting. Still, the little boy was sure that Mr. Flash had been eaten while bravely trying to save the layers, so the little boy could still have his fresh eggs for breakfast every morning. (It was one thing to be murdered, and quite another to die a hero.)

Later that day, after the little boy had safely collected

the eggs from the henhouse with no fear of injury, he went on a walk with his mother and baby sister down the long dirt driveway to the mailbox. On the way, the little boy noticed a pile of poop in the center of the lane. He ran ahead to investigate. Sure enough, it was still warm; the boy let his hand hover over the pile without touching it. He picked up a stick from the side of the road and began poking at the poop, breaking it apart to inspect its contents. He saw seeds, some grass, and a few whole half-ripe blackberries. But then, there it was. Right in the middle of the biggest poop was a beak! The boy was triumphant—the fox had done it, and shat out proof.

I have tried my best to avoid the French parenting books, the ones detailing calm dinner parties with mild-mannered children eating their chicken neatly at the table. It's so easy to be sold perfection, and even easier to feel your version doesn't come close. But I have a French friend who told me French kids don't sass because their parents aren't afraid to use corporal punishment. That made me feel better, even if it isn't true. I remember when I was five, my nanny took me to the mall, and when I introduced her to a school friend as my maid, she slapped me. From then on, I did whatever she told me to, and I liked it. She used to give me sips of her hot coffee, which was mostly milk and sugar. She taught me to dunk my bread.

I don't speak French. I've always wanted to but never learned. Somehow, though, I have a perfect accent, and I know basic phrases from my childhood, when my parents took me on vacation. "Je voudrais un sandwich au fromage," I beg my children theatrically. "Je suis très fatiguée," I say, and I know what that means, by the way—it means get the fuck off me, I just woke up. My favorite book is something I found at a yard sale in the free box: *Des femmes dans la maison: Anatomie de la vie domestique*, which means "Women in the House: Anatomy of Domestic Life." I flip through it often. On the cover is a small cutout square revealing a high heel and a muscular leg in fishnet tights. The cover opens to reveal a full-page photo of a woman in her kitchen spraying something from an aerosol can onto her other shoe, her legs crossed, the black sleeves of her baggy sweater rolled up to the elbow, her curly mass of hair, her prominent nose, her big mole, her casual smirk. She wears pinstripe Bermuda shorts over fishnets and doesn't give a shit about the dishes piled in the sink. The writing in the book I never bothered to translate. The photos, to me, say it all: portraits of women named Anne, Anne-Marie, C., Catherine, Josiane, Régine, and Roseline; unfussy women, beautiful only in their haste, in their uncurated living rooms and messy studios, with their tabby cats. They're writing on the shower wall in eyebrow pencil, wearing bifocals and lighting up a cigarette by the typewriter, making espresso and helping with their daughters' homework. They're in bathtubs with their children, using the handheld shower nozzle; they're cleaning their feet, getting out onto shabby bath mats, blow-drying their hair, pulling it straight out to the side of their heads with a brush so their faces stretch. In these portraits, there are warty lips and lipstick application, tables covered with breakfast in the garden, cheesy floral wallpaper, coffee sipped in rumpled bedsheets, and a big-bottomed lady leaning over a drafting table, her cat curled up on the folding chair. I love these women. They are my heroes.

———

The other day I was doing something on my phone. I knew I should have been focusing on the leaf rubbings I had planned to make with my son, but I was distracted. Phin asked me in his high, crackling voice: "What does 'complexion' mean?"

"The way your skin looks and feels."

"What does 'attend' mean?"

"To go to something. To be somewhere."

"What does 'selfish' mean?"

"To think only of yourself."

"What does 'grief' mean?"

"Uncontrollable sadness that never ends, only changes."

What is my sadness? My mind races, and my thoughts are jumbled together like the random detritus at the bottom of a purse. That I am more like my mother than I wish to admit. That I have been set on a treadmill and it's moving too fast. That my kids can't be sheltered from the shit of the world. That my daughter might be raped in an empty parking lot. That my son will benefit from a culture that degrades women. That both could be killed in a shooting at school. That one of them could be the shooter. That we are being recorded, so algorithms can sell us things we don't need. That I've lost my last chance at living in northern Italy as a twentysomething, riding my bike around, diving into lakes; that I have enough money to craft a certain type of vacation fantasy but not enough money to actually act on it this winter or next winter. That even if I changed my mind about wanting kids, I couldn't erase the fact that I have them already, that I'm trapped, that I'm responsible for them, and that if I left them—which I just did—I'd be a horrible person, and everyone would say so, and I would never be able to escape the pain of both being a bad mother and being without them, even if I got on a plane and went to Italy and never came back.

———

"Things I Am Good At" / "Things I Want to Learn"

These are the headings of documents on my computer that I constantly add to, in secret. Surprisingly the first list—"Things I Am Good At"—is long, but perhaps that's because it's filled with entries like "filing my nails in the bathroom when the kids think I've left to walk the dog." It's true, actually: my time spent in the bathroom is some of my best. I artfully rearrange the stacks of thin, flat rocks I've piled like cairns on the ledge next to the toilet. Although eventually—and it doesn't take long—one of the children bursts through the door and slams it against the shelving, rattling my homeopathics, including the one derived from the saliva of rabid dogs, which I take on airplanes because I'm terrified.

The second list is harder. For "Things I Want to Learn," I have to be able to identify what I don't already know, and most of the time I'm making the kids' first snack, then breaking up a fight, then making the second snack, then checking my email for no reason, then acting as a human shield for the never-ending game of chase, which usually ends with a table corner to the head. In between, I can squeeze in a squirt of glitter glue, a couple of picture books, some kissing and hugging, and perhaps even a session of emptying the dishwasher (but not without my daughter reorganizing the clean silverware on the crumby rug). I might even be able to FaceTime with one of my sisters, though usually the kids yank the phone from my hand, fight over it, and hang up by mistake. I have to hide the thing in a high cupboard just to keep the peace. Whenever I have a rare moment to myself, I usually end up worrying about the safety of my kids, wherever they are. I think: Can I protect them? Am I protected, too, so that I have the tools with which to shelter them? And what was that sound? I exhaust myself and I get headaches.

Sometimes, while lying in bed at night, I write in my

notebook descriptions of alternative scenarios in which I'd like to live. I think maybe it is less important what story I am telling, and more how I choose to tell it, or how I place certain details next to other ones. Perhaps, I imagine, I could be a Waldorf preschool teacher who wears only green and purple, with her hair up in a tortoiseshell clip, or I could be a semiprofessional skier who works nights organizing labor strikes, or who makes a killing selling weed, which changes the fantasy entirely. Usually this new life is a direct response to someone I've just met or heard about, after I've expertly idealized their reality as far more interesting than mine. I see the objects they own and I invest in them a significant meaning—a red sweater becomes a symbol of freedom, of museums, of the fresh baguettes I so badly want under my arm. I've begun a new list, titled "Working on My Look," with bullets of all the things I want to buy but never will. The primary inspiration for that one was the wardrobe of a young novelist I saw on YouTube; she was wearing cotton socks covered with paw prints and a pleated skirt that she had fanned over the arms of her chair. She was interviewing a Pulitzer Prize winner—they were joking about book clubs, how they detested them.

Right before I got pregnant with Phin, we saw the listing for our house. There was a Scandinavian feeling to it, like an illustration in an Elsa Beskow book. The roof was pitched at sixty degrees, and although I didn't know much about construction, I did know that such an angle was rare. There were lilacs as tall as trees lining the driveway, and two had been pruned into an arch over the dooryard. There was a pond, an orchard, pastures, and an established asparagus bed. It was too expensive for a couple of homesteaders, but Asa agreed to see it with me—just to gather data, he said. Even the realtor told us the sellers were trying to get top dollar for it in the hopes that some wealthy person would consider it suitable for a getaway. But the house was too far from the ski resorts, and there was exposed electrical that hadn't been dealt with, and the second bathroom was just a toilet in a converted linen closet at the top of the stairs. The house had sat there, slowly lowering in price, while Asa led me by the hand from showing to showing, ticking off all the other, more affordable possibilities for how we could construct our life together.

Imagine this, he said when we stood in the Victorian fixer-upper, with its peeling, light pink paint. The kitchen was such a dump that the seller had left a laminated sign telling buyers to tear it out. The bathrooms were also bad, and the hillside behind the house looked as if it might slide right down onto the wooden deck with the next rainstorm. Imagine this, Asa said, and he showed me a space between the stairwell and the front door that could be walled off, and other places where doorways could be opened. He jumped up and down lightly in the attic and the floorboards squeaked.

Imagine this, Asa said, as we approached the gambrel-roofed farmhouse in the center of the college campus, which shared a clump of ornamental berry bushes with the faculty lounge. The house had elaborately lit exit signs, all to code. Asa stood at the top of the stairs and held out his arms. "This is where the rental apartment could begin!" he said. "And here's where you'd put in another kitchen. Alma, look!" He pointed to the south-facing windows of what was then a living room. The realtor had been following him around as he gesticulated, impressed by his enthusiasm, as I muttered under my breath. She had given us the first look at the house, she said, but it would be listed the next day. She told Asa he had good ideas. "Don't steal them!" he said, and then looked at her name on the listing sheet in his hand. "Don't you go and steal my ideas, Pauline!" And she promised she wouldn't.

I imagined the kitchen where he had told me to. There was a three-sided window seat, and we could leave the groceries right over there. He walked me over to some bay windows. Would I be okay, Asa wanted to know, giving the better windows to our tenants? All I could think about was how we'd need to cut down the lot's only tree to grow a garden.

Asa took me to another house the size of a cat crate. Imagine this: at least the yard was large enough to play catch. We saw a cape with charred cedar siding and six picture windows overlooking a lake, but it was a part of a homeowner's association that included a golf course. We saw a custom-built colonial that was once a forest kinder-garten, with willow-bough forts in the back garden. We made a spreadsheet: in the top row we put the name of each property we were considering; in the columns beneath we ranked them on access to nature and to culture, on afford-ability, on commute. Imagine this, Asa kept saying, and I felt secure but underwhelmed as he carted me from house to house on a grand tour of our possible futures, each ver-sion making its own kind of sense.

All the while I couldn't stop thinking of the steep-pitched roof of the fairy-tale house. So when the price was lowered for the third time, we went to see it again. Imagine this, I said to Asa, as we sat on the back deck, looking down the valley. I had an apple in my bag and we passed it back and forth.

———

Our house is an island surrounded by snow and ice, reach-able only by the shoveled front walk. Asa plows the drive-way down to the mailbox, where the town trucks take over. The sheep are fenced into the back bay of the barn with deep bedding, and they gnaw on our discarded Christmas tree while shooting hardened pellets of manure into steam-ing heaps, with any luck missing the water trough. But usu-ally they don't miss, and I have to fish out the shit with cold fingers.

Winter is copulatory. We have more desire for each

other. Perhaps it is the season, everyone crowded around the woodstove or the kitchen table, shoveling in shepherd's pie. There is little else to do in winter but chop, pile, stir, slide, and lick. Asa and I find dark corners to duck into: the kitchen, behind the cookstove; in bed, with a sleeping kid adjacent. We become experts at timing. Sometimes I think: Do I even want this? But then I see the look on his face, and I want to please him, and so I am also pleased. The kids take baths in the sunroom claw-foot tub, the passionflower vines snake the windows, and they streak around the house with the steam coming off them, hooded towels flying behind them like capes. Their pajamas are worn at the feet, there are cold beds and heaps of blankets, and finally, when the kids are asleep, Asa and I scissor our legs on the couch, reflect on the day, watch videos on the laptop, listen to jazz. We take hot showers, water the houseplants, tidy up, eat ice cream. Sometimes we wait until the kids are asleep to fight, and then we are at each other's throats in the farthest corner of the kitchen, and one of us will storm away before realizing there is nowhere to go.

On the weekends we sled down the measured slope of the driveway, drink hot cocoa in chipped teacups, eat popcorn made fresh in the yellow enamel pot with the saucepan lid, dusted with brewer's yeast, salt, lots of butter. We get cabin fever. We get snowed in. We don't see anyone else for days. We go to the pool an hour away and pay forty bucks to swim in other people's pee. I tiptoe through the dressing room, sidestepping the tangles of wet hair on the floor. I squat over the toilet like there is nuclear waste on the seat. We come home and everything is so familiar and small and enclosed. There is snow on the sunroom windows and I can't see out.

We skate on our pond or down at the town rink. I bring the kids outside to watch Asa on his tractor as he drags logs from the woods, thinning a copse below the house to expand the orchard. I make sure they don't get too close to any widow-makers. They chase his tractor back up the hill, screaming, pretending to be pirates or bad guys, and we clear off sticks and rubble from the driveway where the trees have fallen as Asa rumbles back to the barn.

Boots on, boots off, fix socks, boots on, mittens on, mittens off, have to pee, boots off, snow pants off, hat off, hat on, pants on, mittens on, fix mittens, jacket on, fix sleeves, tuck mittens under, boots on, boots off, fix socks, boots on. I can't handle the mittens. I am over the mittens, just put on a burlap sack. If I sit my kids on the mudroom bench one more time, for one more minute, to get them dressed for the ten minutes outside until they want to come back in again, I will lose my mind. I think about pushing them, pretending I didn't mean to. I imagine our heat coming out of radiators instead of the wood fire, which burns only in one room and everyone always fights for the spot in front of it and you wake up in the morning and everything is freezing and it takes an hour to warm up. Eden gets a bad burn on her forearm, and for weeks I hear the singe.

Outside there is nothing green. There is only white.

The sky is never blue. Fermented radish smells like farts. Months pass like this. I feel like a sailor with scurvy. We grow microgreens on the windowsill and I look at them and think, It's going to be okay, but then a month later everything is still the same, and I can't look at anyone, because if I do for too long, I start thinking about how much I hate all of this. I read blogs and see pictures of well-lit, plated food with little sprouts on top, while I eat goulash.

In early spring we tap a row of maples that border our property. The kids hold their tongues under the taps to catch the sweet droplets; they test the grade of the syrup by sipping shots out of Dixie cups. They roast hot dogs in the coals of the evaporator, eat them off sticks, race around crazy in the warmer March or April days as the snow melts. We put bands on the lambs' tails and they flick around uncomfortably until falling off a couple of weeks later.

Boots on, boots off, boots on, boots off, muddy footprints in the house. Who invented gloves for toddlers? The moment we've shoved one finger in the right place and begun on the next, the first comes out and we have to start all over again. No one likes their socks. They bunch up, and we are changing socks constantly. The days are longer, and when I count them on my fingers, I can see we are closer to summer than we are to the beginning of the winter. But there is a flood of mud and brown water in the dooryard, and the sheep are pathetic and ratty, and the chickens are shitting on the front porch.

Then, mud season. The car swerves all over the roads

like a jacked-up roller coaster, the ruts sometimes impass-
able. There is nothing but brown for weeks. Crocuses
and snowbells are like gifts from god. We seed out trays
of spinach, kale, cabbage, cosmos, bachelor's buttons, and
zinnias. Dandelions are foraged and juiced, served in pesto
and sautéed. Finally the pastures go green and then, after
months of waiting, explode. Yet I find I've become attached
to the feelings of suppression. I dread the abundance, even
though I know it's better than the dearth. Things start to
speed up, the kids need even more attention, they want to
be pushed higher and higher in the swing.

But then, summer. We turn a deep honey, the kids
run naked for three months. We plant gardens and flowers, raspberries and elderberries, hazelnuts and pears. We
keep bees, raise ducks. Phin rides his trick bike and Eden
chases after him, yelling. They are strong and supple from
running up and down the big hill to the pond. They catch
crayfish, frogs, butterflies if they're lucky. Toads jump on
their feet and are captured, caressed. We cook on an open
fire, make pizza in the outdoor oven. There is no end to
the abundance of the garden. The kids wander through
the hay-mulched pathways, helping themselves to cherry
tomatoes and snap peas, eating the leaves off baby kale,
pulling out a carrot half-covered in beautiful black dirt.
They are mud stained. They shit on the edges of the lawn
and flick it into the woods with sticks. They are exhausted
by nightfall, sweating, splayed out on their beds like drunk
cherubs. Asa and I light a fire in the woodstove on the deck,

and it sparks through the dark. In Vermont the summer days are long, but then fireflies light up the hillside and the warm air is cut by a cold breeze rippling the poplar leaves, followed by the hoots of owls, coyote yips, and the dusk-time tinkling of the warblers. We go to bed late, we wake already tired.

It's manic, the fecundity becomes unsustainable. I try not to yell at guests. I wash dishes constantly; everyone uses a new water glass and leaves it on the counter, and I can't tell the difference between clean and dirty. The dog eats her own excrement. While the garden overflows, the drive to weed it dwindles, and there emerges a general acceptance of decay and overgrowth. The quest for aesthetic harmony is replaced by a fatigue so bone-deep that napping on the lawn outweighs the act of upkeep. The animals are corpulent and lazy. The sheep pant. Hens are carried off in the night.

Eventually, the flies are beaten back by the colder nights. If the heat returns for a day or two, we jump naked into the cold pond, getting leaves in our mouths, the fallen pine needles on our legs like minnows. The numbers dwindle at the town beach as all the summer people leave, and the kids go back to school, lining up and keeping still. The lakes turn murky, the canoes are locked away in the rack, the snack shack french fries have gone rancid. The towels are mildewed, the first wood fire of the season is burned inside, and you can hear the walls shrink. We pick apples and make cider in a hand-cranked wood press; the kids tumble the apples down the chute until Asa clangs the bell from below. Our stores of food are burrowed neatly in the cellar. The blueberries are packed into ziplock bags and frozen, the tomato sauce is processed and put away, the garlic is cleaned and put in a basket. Like preparing for the end of the world.

———

Nature is great, but after the birth of my children I grew desperate to find people who shared my experience— other women, in particular. There was one young mother I turned to in the beginning; she lived a road over and was nervous, obsessed with wool baby clothing and organic bedding that cost a fortune. She thought someone was going through her trash. She was afraid of her neighbors. She used diaper cream from a German company that I'd read had tested their products on prisoners at Dachau. She claimed this wasn't true. I described the biodynamic gardens at Auschwitz, which was over the line, I guess. "I'm not saying biodynamics is bad," I told her. "I love biodynamics!" I had to distance myself from her eventually.

I stopped looking for other mothers when I realized I didn't even have to leave the house to connect. I looked at my phone more, as I had upgraded to a better model. And I subscribed to a literary newsletter, which I read daily. There were many things I became interested in, sparked by the newsletter's suggestions, and at times there were several tabs open on my computer, articles I was reading. By the time the kids were sleeping a bit better, I had begun to read books suggested by the newsletter too. I had amassed a stack on my night table, and I would bite my nails to the quick and flick off little bits as I turned the pages. Each week at least one new book arrived in the mailbox, and I would race down the driveway to see what had come, ripping open the package like an impatient child, holding the book against my breast and tucking it inside my jacket if it was raining. I tried to hide these purchases from Asa, since I knew he would tell me to use the college library instead. But I needed these objects to take up space in my house as proof that I had consumed them, that they were now a part of me. I wanted ready access to the ideas, in case I ever forgot them, like calling on an old friend.

During this period of self-education I discovered a number of writers, all women, whom I had never read before. Many of them had been writing in the mid-twentieth century, some even earlier, and all over the world. Their journeys were linked, some more closely than others. They were part of an old guard of feminists: theorists, essayists, poets, novelists, journalists, truth tellers; some mothers, some not. They spoke of the human condition, of being a woman. Some of them were bleak, and more modern; those were my favorites. They described a world where women were bold and brazen, tormented and out of control.

It was as if a deep cave in me that had been filled with rocks had blown open at last and been cleared of its rubble.

While reading, I felt alone in my thoughts but also a part of something much bigger. These women's words comforted me as if they were speaking directly to me, and at moments through me. They were seeing what I was seeing. Their opinions echoed through the caverns of my interior world. I researched them, read all their reviews, mapped their career trajectories, studied their bibliographies and their awards. I imagined their homes. I read interviews from international festivals and watched YouTube videos where the more recent writers detailed their creative processes in some storage room of a publishing house, their books and the books of others lined up behind them. I quoted them in my notebook. I added exclamation marks in the book margins.

At around the same time, I began to understand on a different level the power of a good story. Every afternoon, as the sun began to set, I put on a video for my children. Mostly Eden couldn't understand the plots, but I chose movies and serialized programming that were appropriate for her—not too violent, not too fast-paced. They were classics, book adaptations, musicals. And while these videos had initially been implemented so I could just get the fucking dinner on the table and have a minute to myself before Asa came home, I realized that the kids now had their own entertainment hour that they reveled in and looked forward to rapturously. In the mornings, we'd sing the songs together at breakfast, as if discovering a memory that had been long forgotten, and my children's faces would light up with the knowledge that I shared in their passion. Asa would look at us longingly; it was these tiny moments that he missed out on, and I saw him wanting more of them.

Of course, I knew that perhaps I had introduced another form of addiction to our lives, that rather than expanding my children's worldviews, I was giving them ADHD. But these familiar plots—friendly witches with dogs riding on their brooms, mice traveling across the world, genies granting wishes, fairies protecting their rain forests—gave my children permission to disappear completely into the warm womb of storytelling, just as I had been. And anyway, the videos, with their quaint dramas and wholesome morals, were not unlike the books I read to my kids at night; each provided a sense of magical wonder about a world that was larger than our four walls. I became certain this was the very magic I, too, was yearning for—a new adventure waiting right around the bend, perfectly packaged, at once dangerous and safe, and as if it were really happening to me.

I also began to tell my children bedtime stories, or, as they called them, "mouth stories." I let my imagination wander in ways I thought they would appreciate. I made the characters familiar enough that my children could recognize themselves. I crafted moral dilemmas to reflect those we all had encountered during the day. Usually I included princes and princesses, animals in human form or vegetables come to life, some sort of "danger." But I never made the stories too scary. At least not right away.

Our nighttime routine took about an hour and a half. Usually I slept with my children—one or both, depending on the rest of the night's migratory patterns—with a set of hands rubbing my torso for comfort, and a set of feet rubbing my legs, as if I were a post for two cats in perpetual itch or ecstasy; it was hard to know which. If I managed to stay awake, I had about two hours of alone time in the dark where I felt like anything was possible.

All I was thinking about was stories. Other women's, my own. My mind was blooming, and so I began writing again—really, for the first time. Lying next to my children at night as they fell asleep, I started to plot things out in my mind: how I could make a narrator braver than I was; how I would give her the words that I could never say aloud; how I could mutate dialogue overheard in the post office and put it in my narrator's husband's mouth, even though my own husband would likely never say it. Asa always fell asleep after a couple of pages of his book, and so I had the nights to myself. I wrote by hand, mostly, in a large hardcover journal with blank pages. I found myself writing about my life in a way that was much different from how I had before, more to understand it as part of a collective experience. I started mapping out a narrative that was more than just my story; it was the story of isolation. Of capital. My main character was a woman like me, her husband was a man like Asa. She had two kids, and some ambivalences about her role as a mother. She was an artist. I even called her An Artist at first, because I wanted her to identify as something I had never felt able to. I wrote without stopping and without judgment, and, honestly, it felt easy.

This, I thought, is what having a creative practice feels like. If I didn't write, I felt an absence. I thought of my mother, who left the house every morning to "go to work," only to circle around and enter through the basement to her writing studio below. I never knew she was there, and I didn't see her until dinnertime. She spent the whole day downstairs as my little feet pattered above, my life curated dutifully by a woman who was paid to love me. Now, for the first time in my life, I understood why.

In writing I found a much-needed detachment from reality that didn't come from daydreaming, or gardening, or looking through old photos, or shopping on eBay. I could say anything, be anyone. I could make up whatever I wanted, even if much of it was drawn from my real life. I could exalt an analysis of my own mundanity that felt, in other circumstances, like whining. And I could begin a sentence based in truth and end it with a falsity so obscene I was sure my neighbors, if they ever read it, would think I was some sort of pervert.

I became filled with a sensation of limitless possibility and of the potential for community. Because if I finished my story, maybe someone would read it. And maybe the world would change—or maybe I would. I fantasized about one day being closer to the literary witches I'd been pursuing and their cauldrons of sensuous discourse, about being legitimately affiliated with them, perhaps even physically.

Maybe, I thought, if we shared a publisher, we would be put on a panel together. Maybe we would be invited by the same corporation to present during a weeklong development seminar, to offer our opinions on the state of the world and the role of fiction in shaping possible futures. I had the thought that writing could be my ticket out of the tedium of rural life; the trap of maternal domesticity and the endless support of my husband, which had taken precedence over everything else; the coexistence with the land that we had chosen and yet that made it impossible for me to do much beyond driving back and forth from school, setting up sheep fence, mowing, moving the fence, mowing again, shaking grain in the bucket.

This is not to say that I didn't entertain doubts about my work. As I read more about my female peers (a term I applied loosely and maybe hazardously), I learned that many of them had struggled against darker specters than the mundane. They had fought more demons than I could imagine. And so I began to wonder if anyone would give a shit about the things I had to say, or whether I was only illuminating experiences that ultimately mattered little. From the outside, I knew, my life looked good. My children were healthy; the food in my root cellar was procured ethically, according to my own system of beliefs; and compared to most, I was bathing in luxury, even if there were spiders in the bath. But my life had felt so hard for so long, and I was beginning to think it wasn't going to improve. My kids would just get older. They'd start driving. There would be icy roads. I'd ask them not to go to the party they wanted to go to. They'd be mad at me for worrying too much. They'd go out anyway. Maybe they'd die in their car. And if I felt like a servant now, how would I feel when my children didn't even want to be comforted by me or held in the middle of the night? They'd want hot lunch at school. They'd buy junk food at gas stations. I was afraid of much more than my husband losing his desire for me. I was worried that even though we were living purposefully against the tides of mainstream culture, I would become abandoned by *all* culture and would disappear entirely. I was worried that I had made children who were self-reliant and in so doing had made myself disposable. I was worried about losing everything. I thought about probability; the way I figured, two kids meant twice the chance that one of them would die young. And while every year that passed was one more year of no kids dying, the odds increased that the next year would be an off year, a year of terrible loss. These innermost fears formed the foundation of my writing, whether I knew it or not.

The story, as it took shape, was fairly simple—it was about a couple living on an idyllic homestead during a time of war. They had inherited money and planned to use it with intention, to save the land they lived on, to reverse the tragedy of climate change in whatever way they could. They hosted important people from far distances, and each party had a "fun" political theme, like "Billionaire Bingo," and the wine was from Europe. I'm sure, in more ways than I consciously knew, the plot I had chosen was my way of coming to terms with the choices I'd made under fascistic governance and the epidemic of complicity that I did little to nothing about (aside from rejecting the most convenient aspects of consumerism). In my story, while the main character believed in the concept of community, she spent most of her energy celebrating herself for being virtuous. In truth, she was a machine, powered by the community itself—fueled by their desire for what she had—peddling false dreams that simply working on the land, or with your hands, was enough to make your way in the world. I wanted her to claim she was struggling, but to have it be obvious there was no end to her resources, or at least that the end was nowhere in sight. My plan, as I had it plotted, was to reveal her true character, to expose her—maybe it was to expose what I feared most about myself. I wrote a scene where she hit someone with her car and drove off without helping. I wanted her to be looked down on, but also to inspire wonder and desire against the reader's better judgment. I wanted the reader to be annoyed by her entitlement, but to empathize with her, too, in the way I hoped to be read if I were written down. The more I wrote about my Artist, the more I realized I needed to create a completely new woman to play her, because I was so tired of myself and my own hypocrisy. I imagined who I wanted to be, so I could play her; I imagined a younger, improved version of my mother, who was taller and better dressed. I called her Celeste.

I had a clear set of requirements as I built my character. Celeste needed to be beautiful but not plastic, with a notable lack of symmetry. I wanted her to have a sense of style that felt timeless, an impatience for trends. She would be a mother, but ambivalent about it, with an affection for the Victorian culture of maternal neglect. And she would need to have a coldness, a kind of aloof narcissism, and an uncanny ability to appreciate herself. In short, Celeste was a woman of privilege—but a "liberated" one, who chose to ignore the harder questions about her life and where her resources came from even as she casually admitted to it if pressed. As a result, she could be happy, if naive. She wouldn't allow herself to sink into the self-hatred and inaction that I was experiencing: the stuckness I felt from adhering to a rigidly cultivated life that no one could see, the trappings of my own choice to do it all myself; the overflow of abundance passed down from my ancestors' exploitation of others, and my subsequent guilt; the sense that all I owned had nothing to do with merit (or at least not entirely); the remorse about the state of inequality in the larger world, something I did little about; and my feeling, as crazy as it sounds, of a lack, even in the face of so much. Celeste needed to be far less worried than I was, about everything. She needed to enjoy herself.

And despite her many faults, I wanted Celeste not to fail as a mother in the ways I felt I was failing, so I could inhabit her success. I added lists in my journal about all the things I had fucked up, and created vignettes where

Celeste did a better job. I made diagrams populating her dinner table with interesting people, and when her children interrupted her, I had her laugh, then answer them patiently. I made her children sleep through the night. I wrote on index cards and taped them to a large piece of butcher paper, to see how I could manipulate their order. If I fell asleep at night with my kids, I would wake up with a nightmarish gasp and work on my project in the dark, using only a headlamp, surrounded by papers, highlighters, Post-its, and half-empty teacups. Whereas in my own life I slid little bowls of yogurt across the table at my children like a tired lunch lady, Celeste would place them gently down while humming; her silk skirt would flutter. And although Celeste wasn't meant to be a perfect mother—she hated being splashed with bathwater, she didn't believe in cutting the crusts off, she had artistic ambitions beyond framing her kids' drawings—I allowed her to forgive herself easily for her transgressions and to continue living. Of course, Celeste was based on me, partially—but the "me" I might have become if I had learned to like myself. I made Celeste complicit in the design of a world that had always been centralized on dehumanization and commodity, but I also allowed her to experience its robust artistic offerings. She was problematic in both her spending and her experiencing, but she didn't care. I was in control; I was both the puppeteer and the puppets.

Spending time in this alternate reality gave me a rush. Through Celeste, I could practice being another woman; I could glow, I could impress, I could arouse, I could anger, I could break all the rules and be rewarded for those infractions. But while I had her silhouette, the details went hazy whenever I tried to look directly at Celeste, and I wasn't sure I had her right, exactly. In the end, she wasn't me, and I couldn't imagine her completely. So I went in search of a real person to use as a model. To steal from.

———

I shifted in the driver's seat; my jeans were going up my ass a bit. Why had I chosen them, when I could have worn something more comfortable? It's because I wage a constant battle with my mind.

Every morning, I follow the same routine: I wake up. I go to the bathroom. When I return, I approach my closet with disappointment and doubt. On the one hand, I'm a mother: I have every right to wear loose, stain-friendly clothing and be valued for my work in the world, not my body. On the other hand, when I got mistaken for a teenager dropping Phin off at camp, I liked it, and wore very short shorts the next day just to get the compliment again. It's like I'm listening to two videos at the same time: one is the video I've chosen to watch and the other an ad, popped up out of nowhere, based on my search history. I can't understand either and they both sound like shit. This is my internal language, what I learned from years of hearing other women discuss their inability to live up to something, taking breaks to swoon over each other's outfits. When I was a child, my mother would come into my room and inspect herself in my full-length mirror. "Look at the way I *look*," she would say. What was I supposed to see? She never told me, but she didn't have to. She needed an audience for her self-hatred, to make it better, or make it worse; she probably didn't know which. And I did what I was supposed to do, in the culture she perpetuated. I watched.

———

I found my model for "Celeste" through an interview on a mothering website. She was a potter who had a studio at the far corner of her spacious Brooklyn backyard, with a kiln. She was successful, a local artisan. She dabbled in cyanotypes and hung the images on a clothesline to dry. She had a woodstove in her studio, and it flickered merrily while her dog napped. She had a big garden with kale plants like palm trees and a carefully pruned wisteria on a trellis. She wore a white collared shirt buttoned to the neck under a slim cardigan and a denim chore coat. She was a single mother. Her family of three was tight-knit, and they had Sunday night dinners with a close community of do-ers and makers. Her walls were falling apart in places, like the rooms in my well-worn copies of the *World of Interiors*. She had beautiful taste in furniture and wooden handles on her forks. She had weaned her son when he was two by throwing him a cupcake party. "I know," she said in the

interview, "it sounds weird." But once she had committed
to the party, made the cupcakes, bought him a present, and
congratulated him ten times on how he had finally made
it—the end of nursing!—there was no turning back. I liked
this story. I thought: I should have done that with my kids.
There were interviews with several other mothers on the
website, but nothing about them interested me. Celeste was
different. She was familiar, in all the right ways. I looked
up her profiles online, her social media. I could imagine
Asa wanting to fuck her. It felt as though I were witnessing
her life through an open window, even though I knew, in
reality, it was only a collection of images Celeste wanted
me to see. But after a few weeks watching, I forgot, and
torpedoed on autopilot through the void.

I had become entirely caught up in Celeste's story, and
in her place in my story; it was more, now, than just research.
I was interested in all the things she was saying and the way
her lips moved in videos, her tongue against her teeth. I
wanted to see more of her objects around the house, to learn
about the ingredients of her dinner. I felt as if I were really
getting to know her. I appreciated her ability to capture the
grandeur of her life, something I could never achieve.

During my private moments without her, I would take
breaks to spend time in my own garden, and I would hear
the birds, I would feel a chill when a cloud passed in front of
the sun. But then I would go inside and pick up my phone
and it would all come flooding back. And then, just when I
thought I had figured her out, Celeste would surprise me.

She would approach a touchy subject so naughtily I felt tick-led in the deeper parts of me. I had a hard time living in the present, but being with Celeste was pretty close, because she was living in it and reporting back, and by association I could too.

At moments it was even as if the writers whose books I was reading were coming to life in Celeste, and so I started to look up to her, in a weird way. I thought it was simi-lar to reading my older sisters' diaries, how their secrets became mine, and I became a part of their world, until they found out and cut off my braid when I wasn't looking. But it felt different with Celeste—she was open to me in a way my sisters never had been. Celeste was offering me the details of her life in a generous way, and she didn't mind if I wanted what she had, if I aspired to the things that gave texture to her happiness. She began to wander into my daily consciousness before my morning coffee and late into my intimate hours. She was something more to turn to, and I pursued the image of her, both how she was in her life and how she would be in my story, like poking at a zit when you know it will only make things worse.

During this time Asa was focused on growing his career and his relationships to his students. He would go to meet-ings he didn't need to just to show that he was serious about his work. We had agreed, years ago, that I would focus on the home and he would look outward—but also that, at a certain point in time, we would switch. When the time was right, he'd said, he would do anything for me. He would move anywhere. If I got a job in Boston or in New York, he would pack up his tenure in an instant. But now I was realizing that I knew of nothing in Boston or in New York that would suit me. What were my skills, even? I wasn't sure I had any, apart from gardening, and the only botanical name I knew was *Acidanthera*. Maybe I could become a kindergarten teacher, but even that seemed like a mountain too tall to climb. I wouldn't last—I was impatient, I was grouchy, I was not a fan of animal crackers.

And in truth, though mothering was supposed to be my area of expertise, I had no idea how to be a good mother. I was not really excelling. I began to watch myself making mistakes I had promised I would never make, and as Phin got more cognizant, they would manifest in his expressions. One thoughtless error of mine that came from a well of self-doubt and fear caused an innocent person to worry that all the love had gone away. I would watch that slow tear drop down Phin's face and wonder if we were doomed to repeat history. And yet it seemed to me that when Asa made any kind of exertion in child-rearing, the world fell over itself with admiration, and when he made a mistake, the same world took no notice. I became angry.

Married life had started to look like this: Why had I used the bread knife to cut the cheese? Didn't I know it would dull the blade? Didn't I know serrated knives couldn't be sharpened? And: How could I have brought home another jar of mustard? We had five jars of mustard! And: You go to the library for books, you don't buy them. There were unread stacks in the bathroom! And: You write down your purchases, you track them, then you tally them up! Asa would follow me around the house, shutting off lights as I turned them on. But then I berated Asa for the way he buckled our kids into their car seats, how he failed to get the mittens tucked under the sleeves of the winter jackets, how he never dressed them warmly enough. There was the cutting board, which was always left out (by him) with crumbs everywhere (he was going to use it later, for a snack, so why wash it?). And there was the door to the fridge, kept ajar (by me) while I brought groceries to the countertop (why bother closing it if I was just going to open it again a moment later?). The days when our lives felt important, paradisiacal, and politically relevant seemed gruesomely far away, almost to the point where you stop believing they happened in the first place.

Three

One day I was out by the barn and the rain was cold. I was checking on the sheep and my toes were ice; I had chosen the wrong shoes, and I was slipping out of them. Suddenly, next to me was the rooster. He was a good boy, and I greeted him, I said: "Well, hello there, old boy." Then that cock attacked me. He spread his wings and rose up and was all over me, on my legs, pecking me, digging in his spurs, and I was screaming and running away, and he was chasing me all over the yard, and as he gained on me I lost a shoe; I had one muddy sock and was running for what felt like my life. At last, I reached the door and was safe inside, where I gathered myself. And then I put some boots on. I got back out there, armed with the sharpest shovel we owned, and I went after him. I had him cornered under the kids' bikes. It was a quick death; I knew exactly what I was doing. It was over in two hacks. Later, when Phin asked me, I said it straight: "He's dead. I killed him."

Celeste would probably just go to the store and buy one of those organic rotisserie chickens in the plastic clam-shells. As for me, I started to think that maybe it would be better for the world to simply have a couple of laying hens, without a protector, roaming around.

———

Even though I was wary of the internet, I gave myself a pass on Celeste. I was just a writer doing research. I was explor-ing a theory, and she was theoretical. But it was so easy in seconds here and there to look at my phone and dip into a world that was overflowing with material. I could scroll through thirty of Celeste's photos while counting slowly to twenty, the kids looking for hiding spots in our endless game of hide-and-seek. Of course, Asa had no knowledge of Celeste or of my interest in her, and I hoped it would re-main that way. When he talked with me about my writing, I spoke in broad terms, hiding behind the abstractions of the creative process.

But when I spent time with Celeste in her story, and then with Celeste in my story, it became more than just research. Her lens on the world was a little like looking in a mirror, like seeing the possibilities of my own life. There were differences, to be sure—her hair was longer and loose, mine was thicker. But I could see that our facial construction was similar, the tone of our skin, the way our hair parted slightly to one side, the rounding line of our lips, how our eyebrows didn't quite reach all the way across the eye. We both cooked with excessive garlic; we both loved jazz; even our window curtains were a similar style, Indian cutout appliqué. The more I thought about it, the more it was true: I looked at her life and there I was, kayaking down a river in Utah; getting my hair cut at a salon lined with walls of mirrors; holding a rabbit in a surf shop in the Rockaways; about to take a bite of a sandwich while waiting for the subway; supporting the more progressive presidential candidate; relaxing after a workout; quoting some saying about loving oneself.

But in her version of life there was no darkness. And in the liminal space of counterpart, I began to weigh myself against her constantly. I anticipated her updates, and when they finally appeared, I analyzed them. And while she made me feel less lonely and less bored, I was also less happy. I was held fast in her moments. Time was measured not in minutes or hours but in the period between her publications. I would swell when she suggested I try out a new bar in Dumbo, even though I would likely never go there. Just reading about it made me feel like I was doing it, or would do it at some future date, and I could imagine myself on the stool next to her, laughing about something, eating olives.

I found myself drawn to her in other ways, ones that affected me physically. That aroused me. Maybe not sexually, or, if so, I never acted on the impulses directly, other than the moments when I saw her doing things that in reality Asa was doing on top of me. But I was also a respectable person. I cleaned, I was present with my kids, I organized their toys, I took them for hikes, I supported my husband, I wrote comments on his essays, I made dinner.

When I was really honest with myself, this much was true: I fixated predominantly on Celeste's beauty. I wanted to solicit someone's opinion. I wanted to take a photo of myself, put it next to a photo of Celeste, and ask who was more impressive, more attractive, more authentic, and have the answer be "You." One day I got my wish. Phin caught me looking at her photos—Celeste was frying up steaks in a cast-iron pan and laughing in a cowboy hat and boots. He said, "Mommy, is that you?" I was so happy. That night we had steaks for dinner.

What impressed me most about Celeste's beauty was how effortless it was. She was so at ease with herself in the world. I was reminded of the framed portraits on my wall, the relatives I passed every time I walked up or down the stairs, the arrangement an homage to their grace and elegance and strength, and to the features that I had succeeded in passing down to my own children. They were women who made me proud of my lineage, inspiring me to be better, as they had been, struggling against the confines of what their culture had to offer them. The rounder bodies, the softer edges, the structured clothing cinched at the waist, the blazers and the loafers, the hats with veils; the woman holding a child on the banks of a river, hair blowing in her face, limbs folded, the child's curls. Celeste had already been granted the gift of ravishing representation that I had seen in these family portraits, that I was looking forward to achieving late in life, or, more likely, long after death, when my photograph would be taken out of a dusty box and hung on its own wall of old pictures. Unless it was ridiculed and replaced in the box—but then maybe the box would be sold; maybe someone would acquire my portraits at an estate sale, maybe they would cut me up and use me in collage.

At this point I was being stretched to my limit when it came to mothering. I tried to access a feeling of selfhood from small bouts of writing, daydreaming, and painting. But after the initial sensation of rebooting with these acts of self-preservation, or self-realization, or self-actualization—whatever they were—when my limited time was up, I found it increasingly difficult to shift gears and return to life as usual. I was even more exhausted in the morning when I'd stayed up too late at my computer. The barn chores felt even more daunting. The children even more parasitic. My home even more of a prison. I couldn't write a word anymore without wondering what a future reviewer would say about that sentence, or if the parents at Phin's school would think I was a freak, or how an advance, even a small one, would split and if that would guarantee my financial freedom if, say, Asa did leave me. I stopped taking pleasure in art as an escape or a way to express myself. I began to see it as an oppressor, asking me for something, forcing me to give until there was nothing left for myself. I gave up on my story, but almost as an afterthought, since it had already given up on me. At that point, when I was granted the rare hour or two of time for myself, I became immediately overwhelmed with fear and discouragement because the worst had happened: I had no idea who I was anymore, or what I liked to do.

But Celeste traveled to Bali, to Mexico City. She captured moments of political unrest on the street. She played the harmonium. She had a friend who won an award, and she wore a head wrap to the ceremony. She was a swimmer. She was sent a birthday cake in the shape of a shoe from a designer friend. She was a trained linguist. She was a good citizen. She asked us to boycott things I wanted to be against. I went to the website of an organization she supported and signed their petition.

I studied Celeste's photos in secret so often, pretending to be emailing and swearing at our slow wireless, and, after looking at her images one, two, three, ten times, would scroll backward in her timeline enough so that I began to recognize her memories and would summon them, instinctively, when something in my own daily life felt oddly familiar. And in the hours between news of Celeste's experiences I waited impatiently. It was like any good story; I wanted to find out what would happen next. It was agonizing to wait.

I watched Celeste from afar, but also from very close-up. It became part of my morning routine; I'd check my email, the *New York Times*, the weather, then Celeste. And my afternoon routine: feed and water the sheep, garden or clean, make some tea, then spend time with Celeste. I wasn't even sure I wanted to be doing it anymore or why I was doing it, but I was doing it and I continued to do it. I caught myself saying her name aloud in my car when I was alone, to hear how it sounded in my mouth. And while the act of inspecting her was with the deeper intention of improving myself, it had started to feel more urgent than any new idea I might find in a book. How could someone be so blind to her own vanity, I wondered. But then again, I was jealous of her blindness. I zoomed in on photos to study her pores.

She wasn't all problematic, though, and that confused me, especially when she admitted to softened versions of what seemed like despair. I began to see hints of the deeper, truer part of myself in Celeste, and with my admiration of her life and the way she presented herself to the world came an occasional appreciation for myself. I discovered through her an all-woman Malian band, and I listened to their music often, dancing freely in the living room. And when Celeste brought home sorrel from the farmers' market, I made the same salad she did, relishing the lemony flavor of the greens I had ignored for so long as weeds in my own garden.

I had been isolated, but through Celeste I was seeing the world. And as her experiences piled on top of one another in my memory, over time they eventually became mine. She offered me her shell, and I could hear the ocean. And while I still felt like the copy to her original, at times I could imagine that if I took a picture of myself lying prostrate on a sofa wearing a bathrobe, I, too, could appear heavenly, that someone somewhere could think me a goddess. That the basket of eggs I was carrying, the handful of zinnias, the bushels of dirty potatoes, were symbols of my own accomplishments, my own success. I wasn't far off. I wasn't there yet, but I wasn't *far*. And while I had always been aware of my own humanity somewhere inside me, Celeste brought what was buried in me to the surface. It was fucked-up.

—

Every now and then I reached out for my phone in the dark car. When I found the round button and pressed down, the car was flooded with white-blue light and I could see the seats reflected in both the windshield and the driver's side window, so that my perspective was from two directions, one of them upside down. I pressed the button again so I wouldn't lose the light, and swiped into a sensation so deep it penetrated the density of the car, the pavement, and the earth's crust, into the raw lava nucleus of whatever was beneath. Without looking, I found the page of applications and tapped into a boundaryless zone. I keyed in the letters of her name and swerved onto the rumble strip as I corrected my spelling errors, juddering back to attention. But the road was empty. There was no risk.

There she was, surrounded by a halo of rainbow light

at the Japanese embassy. She was in the bathroom, her dress structured and cinched, sustainably made, the sleeves cut at a bias. Her earrings were a pair but didn't match; one was a gold leaf encircling a diamond, the other a staple. Her handbag was a cube of Oaxacan palm leaves, her shoes velvet with kitten heels, the straps crossing her ankle. Her hair was up, and her skin was damp with oil I could almost smell. The phone went dark, and I set it down again on the seat beside me. I drew in a breath, stretched my chest forward, and arched slightly, my hands at ten and two, hearing a pop in my upper back.

———

Several weeks ago, with the first fire of fall, the woodstove started to whistle. There was a problem with airflow. When I opened the stove door, the whistling stopped, but you can't live like that. I closed it again and tried to cover all the obvious cracks, to see where the leak was. Nothing worked. The whistling lasted for days, and then a week; it was louder at times but even at its softest was impossible to ignore. Its pitch was consistent, mind-numbing, maddening.

I lived with it for a while. I put on music to cover it up. I welcomed the rumbles of airplanes overhead, but they were gone too fast. After two weeks, I was walking around the house plugging my ears with my fingers. I called the chimney people twice, three times, and no one called back. So, finally, I tried to fix it myself. I put a yoga blanket on

the top of the stove and lay back onto it; there were tiny
silver threads that started to smell acrid as they burned
and I knew I didn't have much time. I wore goggles and a
headlamp. I looked up into the chimney and saw it was an
insulation problem. I took the metal poker and explored.
Granules were raining down on me and I was blowing
them out of my mouth, cursing. I used orange scissors and a
stick to stuff insulation back up into the chimney, wedging
it there, trying to remain silent, trying to hear if the whistle
got softer. It didn't. But then it did. It was a miracle; it was
that easy. The silence was like a hot bath. I yelped for joy,
then did a little dance. I swished myself off, dust and insulation flying everywhere. I got out the vacuum. I sucked
up the mess. I put the vacuum away in the broom closet,
and when I came back into the living room, the whistling
had begun again. I was furious. I put my goggles back on;
I was in the dark cavern of the space around the chimney
and the whistling wouldn't stop. I was living on a sled going
eighty miles an hour through the tundra with this sound,
and I was clanging with my scissors against the metal heat
shield, and I was about to stab someone, and my back was
too hot. Phin was laughing, watching me from the couch,
eating an apple.

———

Just for fun, Celeste went on a little trip to a spa in Quebec
by herself. She wanted to spend some time alone, away

from it all. The spa was eco-friendly, the meals grain-free. Every morning she woke up with a glass of Green Tingle: juiced parsley, apple cider vinegar, fresh ginger, and turmeric. She had foam above her lips and a towel around her head. She sipped her coffee, read her book, and her legs were crossed on a padded pool chair. I went to the spa website, and in big letters it said: "Stop and notice how you feel." I felt a yearning. According to information on the website, Celeste's first thermal stage could be to increase her temperature with either the eucalyptus steam bath or a Finnish dry sauna. Then she could close her pores with a brief dip in the Diable River, the Nordic waterfall, or the cold plunge pool. Finally, she could rest her body in the solarium, the firepit, or the zero-gravity pavilion. Celeste had never felt better. She was filled with a sense of self-love, she was well-fed but had a lightness, she was sleeping deeply, she was massaged twice daily, and by the end of it, she had spent less than she would have on a normal weekend out in Brooklyn. She returned rejuvenated, back to life but with a glow.

I, too, had an experience at a sauna, with one of the deans' wives at her rural mountain estate. She had invited me many times, and I finally said yes. We were naked, and although our limbs and curves had seemed utterly disparate when clothed, here in the sauna they were carved from the same stone; breasts were just breasts, knees were knees, a dimpled haunch was obscured by the dim light and faint cloud of steam. At one point I felt a drip of sweat fall from my torso onto my thigh, and for a minute I worried it was breast milk, seeping as if in response to a sudden need.

The dean's wife was telling a story about her husband, who I knew struggled with darkness. When I'd asked her how he was that day, she used the word "discouraged" instead of "depressed." "'Depressed,'" she said, "connotes a feeling of being stuck in a state. 'Discouraged' is an emotion that ranges, day to day, on a continuum." This made sense, and I wondered if I, too, was discouraged. The dean's wife shifted on the cedar bench, and I could hear the click of her knee joint. The previous week, she said, the dean had run over a deer on his way home from work. The road that night was a sheet of ice, and he put the brakes on when he saw the deer. But the deer had stopped when it saw the dean's headlights, and when it tried to sprint, it slipped, and all four legs flew out from under it. The dean had no time to think and drove right over the deer's hind end. At this, the dean's wife brought her legs in and hugged them close to her chest to conceal the rest of her body, as if covering her extremities would make the story she was telling more bearable. "Of course," she went on, "you can imagine he was shaken up, and pulled the car over to check on it, hoping, and really expecting, that the deer would be dead." She stopped for a moment to drink from her water bottle and wipe away the sweat that had dripped into her eyes. "But it was still alive, and it was dragging itself over the ice by its front legs, trying to reach the other side of the road, blood pouring out of its mouth." She got up to pour some more water on the stone slab. There was a loud hiss, and immediately the temperature in the sauna increased as the room filled with steam. I let my body spread out a little, soften with the heat, as the heavy yellow light of the sun shone through the sauna's small window and soaked into my skin like I was dipped in butter.

Her husband had begun to panic, she continued, and could think only of putting the deer out of its misery. But everything was covered in snow. What could he use? A rock? A sharp branch, to stab it? He figured this would likely just increase the deer's suffering. The dean crouched over the deer, speaking to it, consoling it, and suddenly he saw the headlights of an oncoming car, which stopped, and the driver got out to see what was going on. It was their neighbor, the dean's wife explained, who reminded him that finishing the deer off outside of hunting season was illegal, and what with all the blood everywhere there was sure to be an investigation, and if the dean tried to kill it, he would be slapped with a nasty fine. One could not, the neighbor said, use the excuse of ending an animal's suffering, as it muddied the waters between good Samaritans and the lazy fucks who shot deer from car windows (also illegal) and then ran over the dead animal, claiming the latter incident had preceded the former. This was the worst kind of irony, we agreed, sweating on the cedar seats. She continued the story—in the middle of the discussion between the dean and his neighbor, another car stopped along the side of the road, and a young man got out to join them.

The deer was still fighting for its life, she said, shuddering and moaning, and the amount of blood had increased so much that everyone was sure it would die at any moment. At that point, the young man pulled a handgun out of his jeans and scratched his head with it. "There they were," the dean's wife said dramatically, "standing with their hands in their pockets in the dark, as the deer heaved and struggled against the weight of its pain." She apologized to me for the nature of her story. But what happened? I wanted to know. The neighbor had called the game warden, she explained, who, luckily enough, lived close by and was headed in that direction anyway. She fed another log into the stove. The temperature in the little room instantly went up again and removed all barriers between our bodies and the air around us; we were now turned inside out and sweating hard.

I asked her if the dean had left the deer alone, and she confirmed that yes, he had, in order to make their dinner engagement. She said he had since gone down an internet rabbit hole, and just this morning had asked her to change the wireless password and not tell him what it was. She said it took him forever to get places these days, since he had taken to driving way under the speed limit after dusk. When I asked her what he was searching for online, she said, "Just the usual stuff. But one thing leads to another until, all of a sudden, you're somewhere that feels dangerous."

One night after dinner, Asa told me about a class he was teaching on fairy tales, which he referred to as mankind's first tutor. He was doing the dishes, shirtsleeves rolled up to his biceps, and talking about our inherited mythologies and how we reuse them for generations, editing and adapting as we go. He said perhaps it is the writer's duty to record cultural shifts and offer them as representations of reality, in order for new metaphors to take hold in the collective unconscious.

He told me the classical stories we draw from all have roots in the male quest for dominance. And perhaps the reason we are so interested in retelling them is the hope that a newer permutation will somehow make the underlying truth more bearable, that those in power want to use people for their own gain. He mentioned one of his favorite writers, who believed a story could never be finished. This writer published two versions, years apart, of his best-known short story, about a honeymoon. The second version was very similar to the first, but the ending was more nuanced. Asa had read them—both were good. Perhaps, he speculated, it was only when both stories were seen in tandem, not just one or the other, that they could fully illuminate the writer's truth; perhaps layering over time was the only possible way to capture the intricacies of deep experience. This was true, Asa said, about fairy tales and myths in general. Because they had been spoken for centuries before ever being written down, they had been modified with every telling.

I had wondered about this, to some extent, while telling bedtime stories to our children. To me, a good story came from the accrual of details, but in reality, for our kids, the ending was most important. It didn't matter how brilliant my descriptions were, how intricate a plot I'd fabricated, or how theatrical the dialogue became. If the ending was bad, my kids—mostly Phin—remembered the whole story as bad. But a mediocre story given a great ending, and perhaps a clever joke, would be considered excellent, and they'd beg me to repeat it the following night. In fact, I told Asa, when I told a "good" bedtime story, and we inched in close and warm and the kids were satisfied, I felt that even if I had made an error in mothering during the day, I could be forgiven. For in the dreamy abyss of our children's worlds, it grew all the more possible that I would present as the good mother, not as the evil queen trying to ruin their lives or kill them, which was my fear. I was certain my ability to tell good bedtime stories had become my best quality as a mother. Asa asked me why I didn't write the stories down. To be honest, I told him, I had never thought of it. I didn't think they were useful, I supposed, and usually I forgot the plot points within a few hours.

But the next morning I saw an advertisement offering the chance to reconsider my position, served to me on a platter by an eavesdropping deity. It was from a Vermont-based toy company, which produced all its goods in the United States from environmentally friendly materials. They were looking for someone to write and illustrate a

book based on some of their popular stuffed animal characters, a book that would explain the deeper issues of ethi-
cal living to children and parents who might be newcomers
to environmental ideology. It would be used as marketing
material, given away for free with any purchase of the
stuffed animals. I applied immediately, without thinking.
And by the end of the day I received a response from their
marketing director. There was a sizable budget and a short
timeline, and they were interested in me.

When Asa called to check in about dinner, I read him
the ad, and then the email offer. There were the numbers,
plain and simple: $40,000 for three hundred words and
ten illustrations. Forty thousand! Asa laughed. "Alma," he
said. "This is your moment."

I became excited; here was a new chance for me to
write, and this time I would be paid for it. The fee seemed
absurd, but already I was calculating the cost of good wa-
tercolors and thick paper. I would get one of those brush-
tipped ink pens. But then, through the haze of excitement, I
thought about the opportunity from an outside perspective.
And I thought: This is stupid. Using nature to get people to
buy things they don't need.

I wrote the marketing director back and asked for more
information, and because I had no stake in the outcome
(or so I told myself), I barely read my email through before
I sent it. Almost immediately I received a response, with
guidelines: the plot needed to follow two of their more popular characters—an owl and a raccoon, with appropriate

wildlife facts included—and their journey to save their forest, which was rapidly disappearing. The company was in a
rush to get the book out. And their reach was remarkable—
over ten thousand copies of the book would be printed and
sent to their accounts, which, they said, had been growing
exponentially since the animals were introduced five years
before. And although the book wouldn't be offered to the
trade market, it would be sent with boxes of stuffed animals all over the country, and mentioned on shelf talkers
in Target and Costco, and unloaded with other purchases
in people's homes, and thrown onto a countertop and quite
possibly looked at by the person who had bought the animals, who might have their mind changed around issues of
environmental stewardship, who might even read the story
to their child as he or she fondled their new toys. Maybe
Asa was right. Maybe this was my moment.

I did some sketches that evening. The raccoon was
cute. Inspired, even. I giggled as I worked. It was like rob-
bing a bank. I felt like an outlaw. I could hide some sort
of message in the animals' dialogue. I could turn it into a
political act. This toy company was, after all, trying to answer the questions of environmental degradation by para-
dox—producing more of the wasteful product, just a better
version of that product that was slightly less wasteful. But
at the same time, there were worse ways to make money.
It wasn't like the toys were made in China, for example.
And what was wrong with children being bought a birthday present, or getting a gift for no reason? Maybe my own

kids would appreciate my attempt at connecting with their toy universe, and they would likely benefit from some free goods as well. Really, how could I say no?

Still, I was unsure if accepting their offer meant, finally, that I would never create a work of art with meaning. I would be trapped forever in the vortex of marketing and sales, and I would never be taken seriously in the literary world. Like, if you searched my name online, stuffed animals would come up. I would, in a sense, become a toy. But then again, maybe the book could turn into a career. Maybe there could be a series of books, or an animated video spin-off. The company's spokesperson was an actress I had always admired, and the marketing director told me she would possibly narrate an audiobook. That sounded promising! But then I would have to say at potlucks: "I work in children's entertainment." Although, when you thought about it, wasn't that what I already did anyway? I submitted my illustrations and an outline of the story. The company loved it. They sent me a draft contract, which I printed out and set at the farthest corner of my desk. I didn't sign it.

Asa was adamant that I move forward with the deal, and he kept checking in with me about it. How else was I planning to make that kind of money? How could I turn down the offer of remuneration for my art? Wasn't I a painter? Wasn't I a writer? Wasn't this a job that required painting and writing? Wasn't the company a reputable one that cared about the planet? It was true; I couldn't deny the facts. And yet I felt self-righteous as the naysayer, and I enjoyed the shamed look Asa gave me when I told him he only cared about the money. "Where are your standards?" I asked him.

But even still, I began to brainstorm, and every night that week, after the kids were asleep, I sketched the owl and the raccoon—the hollows, the tablecloths on the maple-stump tables—and played around with possible narratives. I was brought back to a time when I was a child myself, when drawing had been a central component of my daily ritual. I remembered the shape of the eyes I would draw, the simple one-line flourish of a hairstyle, the ability that came with just pencil and paper to create worlds where I had total power. As a girl I had gone through phases of illustration that roughly matched my development: first there were fairies, then unicorns, then death scenes and daggers, ominous aliens, lions that devoured their prey. Then a longer phase depicting girls I hated spanking boys I had crushes on, and other lurid sexualized vignettes of revenge that resulted in my notebook being confiscated by the teacher and my mother taking me to a therapist. All of this came back to me as if I had recovered from a long bout of amnesia, and I found myself comforted by the act of drawing again, blanketed in an innocent and mindless satisfaction as when stacking wood.

I showed my sketches to Asa, who was happy I hadn't given up. He commented on their precision, the animals' expressions and little outfits. "You're so talented," he told me. I was really good, he said, at so many things.

———◠———

In college I had a writing professor who taught me his theory of the novel. This professor, who identified primarily as
a critic, was self-preserving but not in an overtly offensive
way, for he understood oppression at a certain level and
was empathetic to the human condition. He was Jewish, for
one thing, but had grown up assimilating at a time when
that was considered a betrayal to his people, who, only two
generations prior, had fled the camps with nothing. This
professor was scrawny in stature and once told me how he
was so poor growing up that he wore girls' hand-me-down
pants. He had worked for a long time as the director of
a prestigious literary nonprofit, one that did a lot of good
in the world, which had helped secure his job at the college—a position he was grateful for, yet also viewed, as if
from a distance, as an objectification of his own progres-
siveness in the interest of the college's optics, since it had recently been accused of perpetuating and even encouraging
an aggressive culture of binge drinking and misogyny. The
professor, however, seemed protective of the hierarchy that
held him in such high esteem; without it, he seemed sure,
there was little difference between him and the brilliant
mechanic he loved to get lost in conversation with, the one
who quoted Kropotkin while changing out his oil.

My professor was adamant that good novels put on a
show for the reader, a kind of "fake event," as he called it,

that a reader could experience immersively, as if watching it occur in real time. To him, voice was less important, and was an easier and lazier reach, which young writers would rely on and use as a crutch. Theater, on the other hand, was harder to pull off, and ultimately, in my professor's opinion, it was drama that made a novel good. He acknowledged that excellent literary fiction needed both—drama and voice—and that without the latter, you got commercial fiction, which lacked depth. But we were to avoid telling a story with voice alone at all costs. We were not writing blogs, after all. We were to show *and* to tell, to think of writing as directing a troupe of actors—did they know where to stand, did they have "business" to attend to, did they have a drama to act out?

The novel, he said, was historically speaking a relatively recent invention, preceded by other literary forms like oral storytelling, fables, myths, poetry, diaries, and letters. In fact, he said, the novel was originally invented to help bored housewives pass the time. And until the men took over—he said this apologetically, as if he knew what he was saying was potentially rife with missteps—the novel was a lower form of domestic art, used *solely* to entertain, which played to those women's lack of intellectual capacity (this last part my professor didn't say outright, but the implications were obvious). He seemed to know of few women writers beyond Virginia Woolf, whom he referenced here and there, always with an air of regret, as if she were the only woman writer in history of any relevance.

The professor wanted us to approach our writing with this in mind: In walked Bob! What did Bob do? Where did Bob go? What did Bob say? But I was more interested in thinking about the woman dusting the clocks on the mantel, or the little girl picking at the frills of her socks, and thus I left the class with a bad grade and a feeling of discouragement and confusion, searching for a major that seemed to better answer the deeper questions of what it meant to be human. I should have studied more philosophy, I said to Asa. Philosophy, he responded, struggled with the same disease.

Four

Asa and I were married at home in August. I was six months pregnant. The sky was blue, with only a few clouds; the wind was crisp, the sun was hot. It was one of those perfect days where heaven and earth are interchangeable and everyone is convinced there's nowhere better in the world than that place at that moment, and they're probably right.

The ceremony began at four, and as the guests arrived, they dropped off their gifts—plates of food—under the striped tent by the house. They made their way up the hill in colorful clothing and dirty boots, to where the horses and cows usually grazed. There we had laid out hay bales, each covered with a cloth, and a harpist played as Asa and I walked out from the house. We had written poems, and our friend officiated in a white dress with a blue sash.

My dress was laundered and line-dried white cotton

that cut low beneath my shoulders, billowed out into short sleeves, laced in crossties down my lower back, and folded in whipped cream layers to the ground. I was simple, old-world, mysterious, ripe like the stuff of a first wet dream. I wore a willow crown that I had cut and woven that morning and held a notebook, which served in theory as my cue card for the ceremony, but was in truth mostly a prop to turn to as a distraction from crying.

After the ceremony we went back downhill to the reception. The children of our guests fed the horses with grass clippings, the more mischievous ones lugging over giant sunflowers they'd found discarded near the garden. We served sourdough bread, cheese, hard cider. A friend played bluegrass guitar on our porch, and every so often Asa and I would duck into the kitchen and cut more bread, get more wine, kiss. As the sun went down and the air became cold, I pulled my hair up and wrapped myself in a shawl, speckled with tiny silver stars, a mug of hot tea in one hand and the other floating beside me as if I were dancing. The little kids followed me around as if they had wandered into their favorite bedtime story. That night we lay in bed braided together like a bunch of soft-necked garlic. Asa turned to me and whispered: "We just saved twenty-five thousand bucks."

This is what you're supposed to picture: a bird's-eye view of an antique tablecloth, a wooden cutting board, fresh bread, fairy lights, the reflection of sky on pond. But you'd be missing the old hippies who were there grilling burgers, the ones who asked to have this dance, the drunk ones who pulled me close, whose wives were watching with their white tennis shoes under their frocks, sitting wide on the brown metal folding chairs, their men who sweated on me and said, "This is how we did it *over there*." Like I was supposed to know what that meant.

———

There have been times when I've almost said "I want a divorce" just to see what kind of look Asa would give me. Would he be devastated? Would he pack his bags as if he'd been waiting for me to say it for the last twelve years since we met, or the six years since we married? Or would he crumble, fall to his knees, beg me to take it back, tell me he'd rather die than spend the rest of his days without me? There have been moments when I've despised him with the fire of a thousand suns. Afterward, usually when he apologizes, I realize I hate him for knowing me deeply, for seeing the shit piled up, the dust piled upon piss and cobwebs at the furthest reach behind the toilet of my mind, and I come to understand it's that kind of vulnerability that binds us to each other in one moment, and rips us apart the next. Like how you fight with your mother. You want her to die, but then you need her to hold you. When she does die, you are free, but you are also part dead. You get the stomach flu and find yourself calling out for her years later.

I'm sure all married couples harbor secret hatred

for each other, whether they eventually separate or stay bonded until their final breaths. Usually, for me, that moment where it all falls apart is hard to imagine. But then we'll have an argument that comes out of nowhere, like when both kids were hit with high fevers, or when Eden got a head injury that could have been serious but turned out to be nothing, or when a deer tick became embedded in Phin's armpit, or when the power went out and none of the headlamps worked, and all of a sudden the lonely and disgraced future doesn't seem so theoretical anymore.

A couple of sentences in a children's book summed it up for me, surprisingly. A brother and a sister bear are cleaning out their elderly neighbor's attic. When they find her ancient radio, they turn it on and discover the magic of bear rock and roll. "As the cubs stood listening to rock music coming out of a radio that looked like a cathedral," the book reads, "they had the funniest feeling about how time works. It went back into the past and forward into the future—but now it was the present." The message being that time moves in different directions, sometimes all at once. I considered this passage to be a bit advanced for its readership, but I could appreciate it, especially after reading it for the forty-fifth time. And when I look "forward into the future," to the day when all my aggressions and asides have piled up to make Asa finally leave me, sometimes it feels like it's going to happen now.

Or maybe it's not right *now* when he leaves, because we have young children together, and it is our shared duty to provide a sense of stability during their early years. Fine; maybe he'll wait until they're adolescents to do it, until they've worn out the fabric of their childhood and have moved on to the trivialities of cliques and school sports victories. I'll be alone, after failing to secure legal ownership of them, and he'll start a new family and all the mistakes he made while being married to me will resolve themselves in his new life, and my kids will prefer his new wife's dinners and her snacks and her ambient lighting in her living room, and their stale memories of early childhood will be reheated by her touch, her smell, her extravagant Christmas presents, while I seethe into old age, my tits sagging into nothingness, with no one to fuck except, perhaps, someone I meet while taking out the garbage, another lonely person with sad, bloated feet. Or maybe I get murdered. Or wait a minute—no. I'm going to move to the city and do everything I couldn't do while married: get some inedible houseplants, for one. I'll get thin and wear tight dresses with glittery bows at the breast, swan around and adopt a lapdog, write something that amazes critics, be the impeccable older woman who inspires younger women to follow their own truest paths even at the risk of breaking their families apart. I will stop composting, because I'll be too busy. And Asa's new wife won't actually be as good a cook as I am, because she'll be conventional.

I take my coffee with heavy cream like I'm on the ketogenic diet. I spread butter on my toast like cream cheese. I see it this way: if I'm going to live each day like it's the climate apocalypse, I might as well enjoy my breakfast. I go to see what Celeste is doing. I am filled with a sense of excitement. What will I find?

One morning, I found her eating muesli. She was adding it to a light blue bowl along with hemp milk, while her two sons ate a different kind of cereal. They were all allergic to lactose. And then I found her in the bathroom, going through her beauty routine. I saw that she used Scott toilet paper, which was surprising. A conch shell sat on the shelf. I found her recounting her practice of Transcendental Meditation. I found her saying things about mothering like "With each labor, I inched closer and closer to a source of divine power."

I went to the store and bought some muesli, and I was impressed with myself when I did it. I waited for the woman at the checkout counter to look up when she scanned it and say: "You too?" I began to eat it, with purpose, instead of my richly buttered toast. The cereal tasted of cardboard flakes, with raisins to mask the taste, and it stuck to my teeth so horribly that when I brushed them later, it was like eating breakfast all over again, but in reverse.

I came to know her home as if it were my own. The fringed fob on her house keys and the leather handbag made by her friends. The liquor she stored on the fireplace mantel because she hosted so many parties. There were at least three tagines in the kitchen. She had grown-up conversations with her kids while she filleted the fish. She was standing in the door to her backyard, black against the whitewashed brick. She was wearing a gray dress and a simple gold bracelet. She was smiling, and some kind of green shrubbery was peeking out of the lower left corner. She was about to go inside. I followed her in.

Celeste was on her couch, reading to her children. There was a wall-length mirror. There were wooden shutters on the windows; it could have been Italy. She went to a book party with a hot dog street cart. Her kids went to a school filled with children from all backgrounds. She said things like: "I went out last night, peacocking." And: "This is just one of many kimonos I've collected." She called her friends "babe." She cared about the supply chain. She was leaning on her stoop railing, she was waving to a neighbor, she was reading the newspaper outside in the city on a Sunday. She was in the middle of the action. I zoomed in on her bookshelves.

———

My oldest sister said that I should be eating less meat. I told her that soybeans are grown on deforested land and that clearing the space for her future tofu killed two generations of monkeys. Both my sisters think I am impertinent and unwise, and they dislike Asa. They come to visit with their monochromatic outfits and their leather tote bags and they tell me what it is to be a mother even though they don't have children. They say I worry too much about saving money. They say that compared to the rest of the world, I am practically a nun. They say that Asa controls me and that I am living his life, not my own. But then again, they are impressed by his woodworking. They are surprised when he makes a soufflé and that he rubs my shoulders as he walks by.

I confess to them that I feel trapped, even when surrounded by the beauty of nature. Yes, my sisters' expressions imply. We are all meant to be unhappy in this way. And they think Asa is out of touch. When he describes his mistrust of money, they say: "You can't be against capitalism; you have a Roth IRA!" Sometimes I think about discussing Celeste with them, but I know what they'd do. They'd try to take her away from me.

———

A chicken becomes meat after the plucker and before you cut the feet off. There's a moment right after its throat has been slit, when its body is thrashing about in the killing cone, sometimes hurling itself out and writhing on the ground, when the reality of death becomes almost too dark to bear.

The way we do it, four birds die at once, and it is a cacophony of drumsticks tapping with no discernable rhythm, their upside-down claws on the sheet metal. The blood is nail polish red, and some clots quickly on the grass while the rest pools into little red seas. Feathers dust the lawn like we've shaken out a ripped down comforter.

Two bodies at a time get dunked in the vat of boiling water, loosening up their feathers. About five minutes later they're dropped into the plucker, a large plastic barrel lined with fat rubber fingers. Quickly, thumpthumpthump, like basketball practice in an old wooden gymnasium, their naked bodies—drained of blood, with their bright yellow stockinged feet—get put on the cutting board at the make-shift butcher station laid over sawhorses. There are sharp knives, a sponge, a hose.

First, the feet come off and are laid aside for stock. Bend a foot to find the notch at the knee joint and hack it off cleanly. Then pull off the head. After the head comes the oil gland, situated just above the tail—cut it out in a U shape and toss it in the bucket below. Flip the bird over and, two fingers below the breastbone, make a slit. With both forefingers open a gap big enough to insert one hand up to your wrist, being careful not to pierce the intestines and risk contamination.

The next part is the insides, hot to the touch. I imagine being frozen somewhere, lost on a hiking trip, at risk of losing my hands to frostbite, and taking refuge inside the body of an animal. (These are the kinds of survival tips I know now; another one is if you lose power, you can light a crayon and it will burn for thirty minutes.) Sweep the inner membrane with the tips of your fingers like you're rubbing a crystal ball, loosening the organs from the fascia just inside the skin. Pull them all out, in one bundle of parts overflowing from a small hand. Separate the liver and the heart for pâté and the grill, peel the lungs off the backbone, spray down the carcass and dunk it in a trough of ice-cold water, then dry it off and bag it.

One night after a slaughter, Asa was lying next to me in bed, reading. I put my head on his right pec and felt his after-shower warmth, the subtle rising and falling of his breath. "You smell nice," I said. I reached under the covers and found his dick. "You're naked as a jaybird." He laughed. I kissed him. His mustache was too long on one side and curled over his upper lip.

"You're still damp, fresh from the shower," I continued. He laughed again—the way you laugh when you want something to end—and told me I was narrating. I was holding him in one hand, limp, while the other kept a finger in my book, saving my place.

I still had not signed the contract for the toy book, and the more time that passed, the more I wondered if I ever would. Of course we could use the money—but we could live comfortably without it too. And the money, unlike notoriety, wouldn't last. Perhaps the book was an obstacle to my happiness, a test. Perhaps I should see it as a challenge to refuse what I didn't value, even at the loss of such a grand financial reward. Wasn't this what Asa had been asking of me all along? I knew that if he had been the one to receive the offer, he would never accept it. But he could hide behind me, pocketing the cash and keeping his ideals while I sacrificed mine at the doorstep of commodity.

Or perhaps my resistance had different origins entirely. Perhaps it was just my anger. Or that I wanted to prove a point.

———

Every morning, Celeste woke up, walked her kids to school, and took her dog to the park. A regular community gathered there, plastic bags hanging out of their back pockets for picking up poop. At nine, when their dogs had to go back on leash, Celeste went home and practiced yoga. She showered. She made a smoothie in her robe and then she dressed. She wore wool socks with holes in the toes; in one, a pinkie poked out. She wore brown button-down shirts tucked into jeans with ripped knees and she threw her head back laughing. She went to the gym and she was self-deprecating about being gluten-free. She sang in a band on the weekends. She had one son with long hair and was wondering when he'd cut it. She took baths and you could see her feet and the pots of lavender flowering in her bathroom. She was getting acupuncture for her circulation. She was really into kettlebells. She went to dim sum with a group of friends. She was meditating for four hours a day while her kids were at school. She wore green sneakers and white shorts. She was teaching a ceramics class. She had sashimi and salmon roe appetizers at the Whitney. She ate raw clams with cranberry horseradish relish at the MOMA. She saw experimental theater in the Village, performed in a water tank. She was selling out of her fall line of dinnerware. She was growing greens in her back garden. She was getting attention for her mugs. She had learned how to create the lightest handle, which fit any hand.

⁓

Celeste. Celeste. I see her standing, golden and ripe, her breasts full to bursting, pointed out at the nipples in soft puffs. Her gaze is purposeful, powerful. She is in control. She wears anklets that jingle slightly as she caresses me, as she traces the line of my body with her finger. She swoops her touch over the curve of my waist, dips down the slope of my thigh, across my belly button, then down. I taste her the way you bite into a plum—at first, tartness, then through the skin the explosion of sweet, the juices running down your chin so you're hanging over the edge of the kitchen sink. Celeste. The color of honey. The smell of almonds and cream, wild rose petals and musk.

⁓

When you're living on the edges of society, there's a razor-like cut to your view of the rest of the world. You are removed from the people who are entering subways and holding handrails and have their socks pulled up over their tights because the streets are cold, the people who are walking through windstorms to the offices where they punch in, or who are serving coffee to the people who are on their way somewhere important. Because on the edge of the woods, there is no meeting for drinks, there is no bistro on the corner, there are no mussels and no fries and no pinot noir. There is only the vista of voluptuous green humps, the lone glider overhead, the hawk being chased by the swallow, the walk to the mailbox, the drive to the market.

I received an email from the toy company asking me where I was. They were running low on time. They needed an answer. But I hadn't thought about it long enough. It was all too fast, too easy. There was a weightlessness to it that I didn't trust.

Five

It had gotten cold, and the air smelled of apples just beginning to turn. I hadn't seen something new from Celeste in a long time. Or so it felt—it seemed like months, but it was likely only a week. And yet I knew that during that week she had been out in the world, having experiences. I wondered why she didn't want me to know. Was it secret? Was she cowering somewhere, overwhelmed with the shame of having failed both herself and the culture she had once thought herself in sync with? Was she doubting her potential, her worth, her place in the world, and worrying what we would think of her if we found out, if somehow the air escaped from the seal?

I tried to follow the thread of what she might be doing through the logical trails I could traverse in my mind, using details from her previous anecdotes and extrapolating them. There were so many possible outcomes that ultimately the exercise proved fruitless, and I was left with the terrible emptiness of not knowing, of not being able to know. I began to imagine scenarios that aroused in me a deep sense of anxiety, because in each of them I was not present, in each of them Celeste was evolving into something that was utterly apart from me. I picked at each fray and pulled it out, until the entire seam was open and in disarray. The worst iteration was that Celeste had found someone to rely on, to confide in, who wasn't me. They were together in a place hidden from view—a farmhouse they had rented, maybe, after meeting at a craft fair and wanting to continue a relationship that felt so promising, like nothing they had encountered before, what Celeste had been wanting all this time but had been unable to find.

And they were linked in their professional goals, in the level of acclaim they had reached, in the fellowships and residencies and grants they'd itemized and then reported on. How they laughed, how they identified with each other's history, how much they had in common—things that I, too, shared, but because I lacked all the other decorations, I would never be invited into their spontaneous incubator, growing steadily into all that I wanted to be.

I imagined them in their sweatpants at the breakfast table, having awakened later than normal—what a dream!—and cradling their coffees, one foot perched against their calves, lost in conversation already, picking up right where they had left off the previous night, when they had stayed up discussing Goethe, discussing simulacra, discussing pleasure, and they had let the fire burn low, because maintaining the cadence of their discourse was more important than going out and getting more wood. Instead, they wrapped their sweaters more tightly around themselves—"they," this terrible creation—until each was yawning with the ribbon of dawn.

It was pointless to underestimate the bonds that women can make, and pointless to assume Celeste was immune to them. The simple magic of connection—the collision of energies even stronger than the pull between a planet and its moon, or the crashing of wave after wave against the coast, pulling minerals back down to the depths, the undertow dragging against the seafloor in a performance of power. My wanting was like watching a roiling pot of soup, its intoxicating odor reaching every corner of the house, yet being unable to taste it.

I made myself forget about "them," this unit that was so separate from me, and went back to imagining just "us." I wanted Celeste to tell me how she dreamed of escaping the city and its relentless demands under which she had become tyrannized. When she did, I would comfort her, and we would plan how she would come and live in my studio, and how she would keep the lamps lit late so when I returned home, there would be somebody already waiting, some warmth.

If Celeste only knew how incredible my house was. She would rave about the softness of the sheets, about my pot stickers, how I made my own hot sauce from peppers

I had grown. How everything I had was fermented, in a manner of speaking. She would see that the beams in my living room had roman numerals carved into them in the old-fashioned timber-frame style; she would see that they were oak, pulled out long ago by a team of draft horses from the woods behind the house; she would see that oak trees were rare in this valley but that our land was covered with them, including one with seven equally sized trunks coppiced from the same stump, like rays of the sun. Seven trunks! She would want to stay forever.

She would remark on how hard it must be to carry our wood in, how the fire could never die out, how it burned for six months without cooling below the point of red embers, how we'd stoke it in the middle of the night during a cold spell and wear socks to bed and sleep with the dog.

And she would love my dog. The beast who snores and farts like a steam engine, whose tumors dangle from her stomach like teats, who won't let us cut her nails and who slides around on the wooden floor as a result, clattering as she walks up the stairs. Who barks for her dinner and barks to go out, because we would probably forget her otherwise. How Celeste would rub her! She would dote on her—she would say, "I never pick favorites, but yours is the best"—and would lose interest in everything other than me.

I always thought loving more than one person cheapened it, weakened its power. I thought we all had a limited supply of love, and that it was better to keep affection scarce and put it on the highest shelf, like a pink diamond with fourteen sides. Before my second child was born, I was convinced there would not be enough love to share, and I worried about the pain it would cause her. And when there was enough, it felt like arriving at a glacial pool in the mountains only to discover it is filled with leaping trout.

Regardless of this fact, Celeste had a life that was separate from me, and this increased my longing for her. While she experienced the fresh air and sunlight, I was banished to Antigone's cave. And like Antigone, I had been disobedient—only my disobedience was in failing to become something of value. And because of this failure, my loved ones would also be punished, because they shared my blood, and so they would be doomed to rot on the rocks and be picked apart by birds and dogs. Where was a sister to defend me? I kept expecting to hear her piercing cry. But there was no one calling out for me. No one cared.

Anyway, my life had to go on, even without Celeste, even in the face of my unworthiness. I had to wake up and make coffee while my kids played with their stuffed animals. Asa would head out early after feeding the dog, and I had to get Phin ready for school and Eden ready for morning preschool.

One morning while listening to music in the car, Phin began asking me to translate some of the songs, which were in Spanish. I did the best I could. I listened to a lyric, then paused the music and attempted a translation. But what did that *mean*? he asked. In one case, the song was about someone considered "hidden" from view, mistrusted, seen as a thief by the police, and I found myself explaining the crisis at our country's border to a child who had barely traveled across county lines. Were there children who were in trouble there? Phin asked me, and I didn't lie. I said yes. And were they put in prison too? he wondered. Again, I said yes, emphasizing that they were put there without their parents. I couldn't think of anything that sounded lonelier. Children? he repeated, sounding afraid. I backtracked. No, I replied. No children. I think you misheard me. And then I said: "Don't worry, it will never happen to you." I couldn't guarantee that, of course, but the odds were in his favor. Still, I saw an expression of doubt in the rearview mirror; I wasn't sure he believed me, just like he probably knew that when you die, it's possible your spirit might not go into a monarch butterfly or a hawk (as I had told him), that instead it might just become nothing, going nowhere, and that everything might not happen for a reason.

That morning, instead of going grocery shopping, I went to a boutique in the town where the college was. I was appalled by the prices—but what did I expect? I saw something chic, a collar cut off a blouse and repurposed as a necklace, for ninety dollars. I saw a pair of sneakers made from crushed red velvet and leopard print, and a top that glittered when you turned it toward the light. I looked around, unfolding shirts, holding them to my chest, then folding them again incorrectly. I traced the fibers of a pair of mesh leggings. A sweater the color of juniper appealed to me, and I took it into the dressing room to try it on. I loved it so much, I wanted to buy it, and I just about ripped it off my body. I left the dressing room, holding the sweater, and wafted toward the register, touching a few other items on my way. I was approached by the saleswoman.

"Excuse me," she said, and I could see in her face she was not happy. She was the same saleswoman who just a few minutes earlier had shaken her head silently when I asked if she thought I could fit into an Italian size 40. She was now holding a pair of the mesh leggings in her hand. She told me there had been two pairs, in two sizes, and now there was only one. She asked me where the other one was, in an accusing way. I could see that she thought I had stuffed them into my bag. "I'm not saying you're shoplifting," said the saleswoman, but with those words, in fact, she was. For a moment I worried she was right.

Then I saw that I had misplaced the leggings in my wanderings, leaving them on the wrong table, and I pointed with the sweater toward them. How dare you! I wanted to say, to defend myself. But I said nothing. I didn't buy anything and left immediately, feeling like a thief. Me, a respectable person! Hadn't I proven myself, hadn't I paid my dues? It didn't matter to her. She thought I was broke—me and my dirty backpack. Because I had to think about the necessity of my excessive tastes, because I had to weigh my budget against my desire, I had presented myself as untrustworthy. And what was I doing going shopping anyway? Had I become the kind of person who threw money around like it didn't matter? What a waste of time;

I should never have made the trip, and I hurried to pick up Eden. The stain of the saleswoman's disapproval was hard to scrub out—I felt like dog shit for a day or two.

———

As it happened, the stories from Celeste returned, and while I was relieved and sated, the more I thought of her, the worse I felt. I weighed myself against her again and again, yes; when I took a picture of myself, I looked at it right away and for a minute I actually expected a photo of her to stare back. I thought, when dressing: What would this look like on her? And I began to inspect each corner of her, looking for her shadow. But I couldn't find her weakness. I suspected there wasn't any, even if there was a frigidity to her. I could hear her hollow, nickering laugh, as she tossed her head like a horse. I could picture the way she chewed her vegetables, like she couldn't be bothered to close her lips around the flesh. And I found myself chewing like that, as an experiment, when no one was watching. But then I longed for her knees. I longed for her narrow shoulders. I even longed for her hairline, although it was beginning to gray. I looked at her from hundreds of miles away and knew I needed to find her darkness, otherwise I would be swallowed up.

And then, a change. Celeste was in a car accident. She was in a cab, she was thrown into the partition, she broke her nose. She hadn't been wearing a seat belt, and her features were barely visible under the black and blue. This was the first time I had seen her in trouble. It was an intimacy I didn't feel prepared for. I was too close. I cared too much. I shut my computer; it was time for dinner, I had no plan, the kids were starving.

Her nose wasn't broken. In fact, I learned the next day, nothing was broken. Instead she was enlightened—all of a sudden everything made sense. The beauty and perfection of life, even in its most banal state, had been enhanced for her. There are moments of benign tragedy, she said, that give us the opportunity to reflect without taking away too much, and this was one of them. She had decided to get back into the law career that she had set aside for years, to deprioritize her art for the time being, and now her purpose was clear. She was putting it out there for all to see; she was really excited. And so she was wondering: Did anyone know of a good nanny?

Something in me was let out of its little cage. Here was an opening.

⌣

Have you ever tried something borderline, just to see how it felt, to see if it fit, to feel the weight of it in your hand, to roll it around like a pair of dice? To fuck with fate a little— open your car door and let your skirt be sucked out? Like the preacher's daughter who's not allowed to dance, who stands in the middle of the railroad tracks and screams, whose eyes go wild as the train approaches, and the screen cuts from her open mouth and her rows of perfect teeth and her tonsils to the roar of the train, the barreling down, the unbearable speed at which she is allowing her fate to advance on her, and then at the very last minute she's tackled to safety by the guy who's with her, who's mesmerized by her, who realizes she's spun off like a top, and they lie there breathing on each other and he's in love with her and she's obsessed with being bad, with dancing, with the trains she seeks out often.

That was me, but I was hunched over my laptop. The kids were asleep and Asa was out playing pond hockey. I was typing her name, and it felt so right to be touching my fingers to those keys, the symmetry of the letters, the feel of the smooth black squares. I told Celeste that I was a single woman living on a small farm. That I'd been taking care of two children for the past few years while my bosses hosted well-attended dinner parties in their barn. I'd been living in their guesthouse, cooking for them, doing chores, caring for the children, becoming part of their nucleus. I told her I wanted to move to the city, that I was interested in alternative education, that I dried clothes on the line, made my own hot sauce, knitted hats, darned socks. That I had a passion for building topsoil. I told her I'd make forts with the kids, in her backyard, in the park. We'd find fallen trees and use them as balance beams. I would help them with homework. We would make sculptures out of cardboard and tape. We would cut real vegetables with real knives. I would teach them to ferment, to make charcuterie. I told her I had a collection of vintage aprons.

I wrote with a fever. After months of nothing, the words rushed out of me, tapped from an open vein. I was certain that I was doing the correct thing. Wasn't this exactly what I had been working toward? Wasn't this the moment when opportunity presented itself, and you jumped on it? I thought of my own nanny, of the epigenetic legacy that I had been ignoring. What if I was meant to be more than just a mother, more than just a writer? What if my purpose was to touch the lives of urban children, of Celeste's children? I was all sprung up with self-importance, like a stapler being loaded, packed tightly with the promise of fun art projects, of walking to the museum, and I was brainstorming, and then, SNAP, the stapler shut on my hand by mistake, and I recoiled and I was awake and I looked at my inbox and it was blinking and it said: "Sent."

I had to switch radio stations to something more upbeat. I was getting tired. My phone buzzed on the passenger seat, and I reached over to pick it up. I had received a new email, telling me about my credit rating, and as I was swiping it away, there came another one, a literary newsletter. I deleted the first but left the second for later, and I turned my eyes back to the road.

I thought about the time before email was ubiquitous,

when people wrote things slowly, in drafts, and reread them before they were sealed into envelopes, when they were licked, stamped, piled, shuffled, then delivered. There was still time, then, until the mailperson arrived at your door, still time until the office administrator picked up your letter from the outbox by the copier and delivered it to the post office. You could still remember something you wanted to say, dash to the mailbox, rip open the envelope, and refill it—or you could tear it up, throw it away, start over. You could revise. You could make a mistake, and there would be time to cover your tracks. If you were desperate enough, you could track down the mailperson going from door to door and beg to be allowed to retrieve your envelope. If you could identify all the marks on it, if you could promise you weren't lying, the mailperson might have let you.

But now there is condensed time, there is just the coursing current of moment stacked upon moment, and there are fingers moving rapidly, and there are buttons next to other buttons, with the total opposite meaning. It is so easy to mistake one for the other.

———

Did I want to be her nanny? My intuition said I did, but when I checked again, it said no. Although I wanted to get closer to Celeste, the moment the email was gone I wanted it back. I was disgusted. I spoke aloud in the bathroom where I'd sequestered myself. What was I doing, who did I think I was, where had this taken me? I was shivering and I smelled foul and I threw myself into the shower and tried to scrub it all off me; maybe I could erase it. Then I got out of the shower and ran to the computer to check my email.

I wished I'd never written in the first place, but I also wanted to know what Celeste's email would look like if she read it and responded. Would she say, "Dear Alma," or would she just jump right into a conversation? Would she use a different color font, would she capitalize? And how would she sign her name? Would she say "Best," or would she use her initials, or would she say something like "Be well," as if she were blessing me? I realized, in the course of these thoughts, that using my real name and my real email address was the stupidest thing I could have done, and that I had to come up with a plan B. I decided that if she wrote back, I would never respond, and I would change my email address. It would be cleansing, actually, to begin with a blank slate, so that when I was dead, no one would be able to search through my emails and see all my vulnerability and all my online receipts, and, I vowed, from this day forward, I would never do anything personal online or write anything intimate in emails, sticking to postcards and sending letters only by mail.

All the lights in my house were out except the blinding moon of my screen, and the anonymity of the dark felt safe. I went up to bed and crawled under the cold covers. She hadn't read my letter yet, nothing was confirmed, my email was still living somewhere between reality and a dream.

This middle space wasn't so bad—but I knew that in the morning my take on everything would change.

Days passed, two days. I was unable to stay with one emotion for longer than the span of a single thought. On the one hand, perhaps I was at a turning point, about to be rewarded for my thoughtful authenticity, legitimized as a caretaker who could bring an earthiness to a concretized world. On the other hand, perhaps I was about to be told that I was nothing, that I was too flat, too broad, too abrasive. My meridians were all tanked up and crossing their wires. I had a sore neck. The second toes on both my feet were red and swollen, and I knew it wasn't blisters, it was a stoppage, it was this energy trying to move, but it was too sluggish, and it was building up pressure so that I had to rub my feet together to relieve it. If I were rejected, if she told me I wasn't good enough, then I would be erased. I would watch the scene of my own dismantlement. I would feel my insides scooped out like melon balls, precise and violent in the bowl.

I waited an hour between glances at my phone. This felt like a significant accomplishment. But then I checked my email fourteen times in the next hour, and when I put the phone away, I felt proud of myself for laying it facedown. Later it was the same thing, tens of times, then a timed hour break, and so on, until I went to bed.

I woke up on the third morning and got to my phone before anyone was awake, but still, there was no response from Celeste, nothing interesting in there at all except a notice from the town about a missing cat. The rest of the day was blurred into one long visit in time's waiting room, where the doctor never came to get me and I was sleeping on a coffee table covered in magazines. Every second felt like a month, every hour like a year. When my kids asked me for something, I snapped at them, and even after they fell silent I continued to admonish them. They wanted peanut butter on apples and I delivered, I achieved a household task, but on the way to the kitchen I caved, I checked the phone again. Nothing. How had I become so invested in this?

⌒

Celeste's world was so decadent, so skillfully aestheticized: the place settings with the rattan mats, the pairs of plates, the patterned napkins, the floral centerpieces. I looked at my own pots of aloe and rosemary, but I could not find the beauty in what I had. I wanted more. I wanted the low light left over from her dinner party. I wanted the terrines, the cheeses, the saucer of olive pits, her gray sweater, her red socks, the glint of gold at her throat, her smooth skin, the glow from within. My own things were dulled, they had no hot bite on the tongue. I looked at a cloth napkin lying on my counter. To wash it was pointless; it would stiffen like a starched flag on the drying rack and I would have to crumple it in my hands to get it to fold.

That night, while waiting for Celeste to respond, I

made an elaborate meal while the kids were watching a movie. I shaved a cabbage into slaw, I mixed turmeric into rice, I made a sauce and slit lemon wedges to balance on the rims of our glasses. I cleaned the pedestal of our heavy oak table, and when I came out from under it, I saw the magnolia tree outside the window framed by the soldered windowpanes, its bare black branches gleaming with a thin layer of rain. For a moment I stood in awe of its beauty. When the spell had broken, I noticed that all our forks were different. Nothing is perfect, I thought, as I lifted my phone to document the scene I had set, to capture how the tree was affirming it, letting the light through. But it was no use—I couldn't include both the foreground with the table settings and the background past the window, it was one or the other; the focus wouldn't cooperate. I had put the last of my zinnias in a vase, and to pick up the red of the flowers in the fading light I had to turn off the kitchen light, which made the rest of the objects seem dark and grainy.

Even so, it was a good dinner. Asa praised me, and Phin asked for seconds and thirds. But there was a part of me that was left unattended, a part that wanted to share the moment, to present it to someone else and have the person respond that I always got it right.

Asa did the dishes and sat with the kids in the bath while I fretted, biting fingernail after fingernail. I thought to myself: Was this an unavoidable system? The desire for extravagant houseplants and a tiered cake with figs? The need to make things better, even when they were already good enough? Was I behaving just as I was expected to, near the top of my ladder, one leg outstretched while I sought out a higher rung? Did a higher rung even exist, or would I fall in my search for it? And what was wrong with just being mediocre? Part of me was comforted to think that if I could only shake myself out of my jealousy, I would be free. But part of me thought that, deep down, I was lacking.

Sometimes when I have been busy working on an index, mired in the cartographic tangle of cross-references, my brain has felt occupied and I have been, in a sense, free from all other desire. That's when I have been closest to a machine; I needed fuel to keep going, but otherwise I was good. It's possible, by this reasoning, that if I took more responsibility, or if I were employed at an office, I would come home at the end of the day and simply have less time, less energy, less compulsion for internal devolution. "Maybe I need to do more honest work," I said aloud, and I heard the words echo in the empty car.

The only company I had was my thoughts and the radio, which suddenly broke from its programming with a request for financial contributions. I had been listening to Bach's *Goldberg Variations*, the host said, and if I chose to give now, I would enable them to continue providing classical music that would elevate me in return. Elevation—wasn't that what I had been looking for?

As I drove through the darkest hour, I saw almost nothing, as if I were on another planet, devoid of human existence. And yet I was not entirely alone. For there at mid-sight line sat Venus, bright and soldierly, to guide me. I was so close.

———

It was 6:00 a.m. on the fourth day since I had written Celeste. The kids pounced on me in bed, and so it began, the shuffle in socked feet downstairs, the endless morning routine of demands and the dragging of chairs from countertop to countertop as they followed me from teakettle to cutting board, begging to help, using the knife upside down and mashing their fingers in the butter. I made it through toast and fried eggs before I checked my phone, and there it was, at last, the bolded subject line in response to my own, our names sitting right next to each other. I touched the screen immediately and saw the message; it was casual but surprised and excited. "So great to get this!" she wrote. "Would love to talk. Tell me more." I threw the phone on the counter like a hot pan.

I had to let it sink in. I was smiling, like I had won a prize. I was shaking a little, too, and some coffee spilled. Now I realized I was actually doing this. I avoided my computer and my phone for half a day. It always happens like that—you get the thing you've been waiting for, obsessing about, needing, but it's there almost too quick, even though it was so late in coming, and you realize waiting for it was almost better than having it.

———

It was three days before I wrote Celeste back. I decided, with some distance, that I had come upon her by very legitimate means, and this was just networking. I was also certain I would never actually be her nanny, even if she offered me the position. I wasn't planning to take it that far. Yes, I had made a mistake by reaching out in the first place, and yes, it was perhaps the most embarrassing thing I'd ever done, but no one else knew. I could easily stop at any point and remedy the situation by saying something like: "Never mind, I've gotten another offer, best of luck finding someone." Then it would be over, and she'd never have reason to contact me again, and if by some improbable chance our paths crossed in the future, I could simply play dumb and say someone had played a cruel joke on me. Or I could say it was research for a character I was writing. Of course! That was the *truth*—I had forgotten this whole time—it was just for research! And anything done in the name of research was perfectly defensible. But even as I found this distance, as I rationalized my ongoing behavior, there was also a creeping back in of the possibility of a new life, the way a strawberry plant jumps the boundary of its bed and takes root in another one. I was hooked by her story in such a way that I couldn't easily be ripped out.

I used my computer, as it was much easier to type on a keyboard. I could control the tone more, could feel the variations between keys. Again I wrote at night, and there was an elegance to my composure, a certain gentility; this was completely okay. I told her I was probably not ready to make a big move, but I wanted to entertain all possibilities and let my intuition guide me. I was attached to a life on the land, but there were performances I wanted to see, people I wanted to interact with. The solitude of Vermont was weighing on me; the community was mythological; in reality life was isolating, each household its own entity. I wanted my email to be intimate, like we were having a chat over a cup of tea. Of course, I knew what kind we'd be drinking: mango ginger, and I would take honey because I wanted to see what she looked like when she got up to retrieve it from her cupboard. I wanted to see her in full extension, from her bare ankles below the frayed cuffs of her white carpenter pants, to the tip of her braid and up her polka-dotted back, to her smooth arm and tattoo of a moon and to the tips of her fingers as they closed around the plastic container. I wanted to watch her work. I wanted to experience our connection. I wanted to make it real. I felt as if in some ways I was already there, already had the mug, was already asking her where I should place the tea bag I had wrung out. It felt totally natural to be in conversation with her, after all these months of learning about her. Now I could really know her, on a human level. It was what I had been looking for all this time, and finally, it was happening. I pressed send. I waited.

Breaking the rhythm of my trance, Asa walked into the room, and I quickly closed my laptop. He was holding up a piece of paper.

"What the fuck, Alma?" he said. He waved the paper closer so I could see. It was the unsigned book contract from the toy company.

"I'm thinking of not doing it," I told him. "It's stupid. I'll become a toy."

"That's ridiculous," he said. And then: "You're crazy."

"Why? Because I have standards? Because I'm resistant to being pressured? Easy for you to say, married to conservatism, all of you." I was making things up as I went; only some of them made sense.

"I'm tired, Alma," Asa said. "You make it all so hard. For yourself. For me."

"Fuck you!" I said, as if to prove his point. I stood up. I went right over to him. I looked him in the face. "You're a goddamn hypocrite," I hissed, and sat on the couch. My sisters were right.

"You're kidding me!" His voice went higher and began to crack. He got that look on his face, the one about the injustice of misperception. He hated to be misjudged. And I wasn't sure if I was actually giving up on the toy book project. In truth, I didn't know what to do—it was a lot of money, and I had enjoyed making the sketches. But I wanted to see Asa's reaction. I wanted him to tell me I was brilliant again and again, that I *needed* to do this project. That I was an artist. I wanted him to beg me to do it. But instead, I yelled after him as he left the room: "You want me to sell myself!"

I opened my computer angrily. Celeste had already replied. "When can we meet?" she had written. And I knew then that I had found it—my purpose. I looked at the clock. I wrote: "Tomorrow."

The kids were safe in bed, and I heard the sound of water running in the bathroom. Asa liked to take long, hot showers, and I noted this as yet another strike against him. I put on my shoes. Then I left.

Six

I looked at my engine light, which was back on. Maybe in winter I would have been more cautious, but that morning I ignored it. I pulled onto a cobblestoned block as the sun began to rise. I had a feeling of purpose and forward motion, but no clear direction in which to apply it. I thought about what Celeste might be doing. Last night she had been at the Japanese embassy. How late had she stayed up? Would she sleep in? Maybe not—it was Friday. But now I was checking, and she was awake after all. There she was on her back deck, drinking coffee in her bathrobe, with her ankles crossed in marled socks. She was on her way to an early yoga class, the coordinates of which I could only guess—but then I didn't have to guess at all, because she posted the name of the studio, and when I tapped it, I could see myself as a blue dot moving on a map. I turned around and got back on the Brooklyn-Queens Expressway.

———

I was in Williamsburg; it was seven. It took me a while to find parking, and by that time, I was sure the yoga class had ended. This was an energetic journey, I said to myself, and energetically there was a large part of me that didn't want to run into her, or perhaps didn't believe it would be possible. Asa kept calling me and I ignored him. He left messages that I didn't listen to. He sent me an email filled with serious concern. He wondered if I was dead.

I needed some coffee. I went into a café with cathedral ceilings, glossy wood stools, a chalkboard menu featuring the dozens of varieties you could choose from. There were six people making coffee with calculated grace; they had been trained for this. The floor was marble. I had no idea what to order, and for a while I stared dumbly up at the menu.

Eventually I chose an Americano. I dug in my bag to pay the cashier. It was now the morning rush, and the line snaked long and winding behind me. But as I grabbed my coin purse, it caught on the zipper of my bag. It was bloated to the size of an orange, filled with quarters and dimes; it had been falling apart for years. Suddenly, coins flew across the room, showering tables and floor, scattered like seeds, and dropping into people's cups. I kneeled and began to collect them, frantically. The knees of my jeans grew dirty as I chased after my money. I had to excuse myself again and again as I crawled beneath the high tables,

and people lifted their legs to let me through. I bumped
my head against shins and handbags. I felt so visible, all at
once, like a cloak had been thrown off. I was sure the other
customers could see my desperation, the bags under my
eyes from the long night of driving.

Maybe this was a sign that I should turn back. That
I wasn't welcome here. But—as with the warning in my
car—I ignored it. And when I had collected my coffee and
my coins, I went outside and saw that the sun was shining
and the air was warming up, and I was in the fractals of
urban life. I found my mind warping around the corner of
a building. I took a break to brush off my jeans under some
scaffolding, and I looked at my reflection in a window to
get a sense of myself.

At a crosswalk, I waited for the light to change and
saw the other people chewing their cud, lost in their own
little worlds. There was a man with a bike chain around his
neck. There was a woman wearing blue lipstick and a spike
through her lip, an old lady with a shopping bag full of bread
crumbs. There were kids in glittered sneakers on their way
to school, a napkin floating by, someone smoking on a stoop.
No one looked at me. It was as if I wasn't even there.

Why did I suddenly feel taller, more substantial, with
a swing in my step? The store windows I passed, which
could have filled me with despair and longing, didn't. I was
wearing my leather boots, molded perfectly to the shape of
my feet. Of course, I thought every so often of my family.
Asa was taking the kids to school by now, and they would

be distracted by their own social obligations. He would go
to his classes, his meetings. I guessed he would pick up the
kids at the end of the day. They'd figure it out. What once
would have worried me felt irrelevant.

Everywhere I walked, I kept my eye out for Celeste. At
every turn, every intersection, every car opening its door,
I thought I might see her. I felt breathless, determined. I
wanted a cigarette for the first time in years, just to hold
something in my hands. And I wandered. In one sense, I
was lost in a sea of millions, with no concrete information
on where Celeste lived or what her plans were. But in another sense, I knew exactly where I was going. I just had to
wait for her to tell me.

I stopped for a moment and checked my phone. Had
she written me back, had she given me an address, a place
for us to meet? But there was no verbal reply, so I went to her
images. There, she was enveloped in a new green sweater,
a gift; she was thanking her friend for it. She presented a
still life of a staghorn fern and a basket and some kind of
smooth rock in the corner of a shop with white walls. I
looked at the location, and mapped it on my phone. I had
never done anything like this before, but it was so simple.

I was breathing the air she was breathing. I was side-
stepping the garbage that she, too, was avoiding. I was let-
ting myself linger over the details that were also part of
Celeste's physical day. And I was flooded with memories.
There was a gallery—was it somewhere she'd been before?
There were ceramic busts in the window like the one on

her mantel. There was a vintage store. I thought she actually shopped there; wasn't there a costume she had purchased? There was a diner in an old Airstream—Celeste liked their mac and cheese. And then the blue dot on the map that meant *me* hovered over the place where Celeste had just been.

I looked up into the window of a little fiber studio. The glass was painted with white lettering, like an old apothecary bottle, and inside were window seats covered in embossed fabric, linen chairs embroidered with roses, and baskets filled with roving, yarn, and knitting supplies. There was a loom. There was the staghorn fern in the corner. I felt a sense of eerie recognition, like I had been there before, and in a way, of course, I had. In the window I saw a hand-knit angora wool sweater hanging from a birch branch. Just like hers, only yellow.

I went in and touched the sweater. My hands were clammy. The price was secured with a safety pin: $195. I had the feeling I was being watched. It was unclear if the store had opened yet, even though the door was ajar. I made an effort to keep my hands visible. The owner of the shop came out of a back room and sat behind the register, making me jolt to attention: "Isn't it beautiful?" She told me the angora was from rabbits on a farm in the Hudson Valley, that she had gone to one of their events just last week. "The farmer is the most *wonderful* woman."

I held the soft sweater in my hands. I told her it was pretty. She replied that it was actually pulled at one

buttonhole and was meant only for display. But then, after a brief pause, she said she would give it to me for 40
percent off, that she thought it would look amazing on me.
My fingers were shaking as I thrust my credit card at her. I
wanted this to be over. Did I want a bag? No, I would wear
it, I said, and I put it right on.

I walked for many blocks, and soon it was noon. The
morning had darkened. Another call came in from Asa,
which again I ignored. I could see rain was coming. It had
gotten colder. As I watched the shapes of people moving
through the streets, I began to feel very far from home. I
checked my phone, but I couldn't locate Celeste. I looked at
my email, nothing from her, then back again at her array
of images. Really, she could be anywhere. I would have
to wait. As a distraction, I thought I would stop and eat
something.

I went into a restaurant with blue awnings and a
Moroccan-inspired menu, round wooden tables and green
leather chairs, and little white bowls piled high with sugar
cubes. The waitresses were wearing structured boatneck
tunics over tights. There was a table available at the window, and I sat there, resting my bag on the window seat
cushion. I ordered whole-grain toast and a tea that came
out on a blue-rimmed saucer with the name of the café
hand-painted around the edge. The waitress brought me a
glass of water. There was a newspaper on an empty seat at
the table next to me, which I flipped through while I ate.
Almost at once the café filled up, and after eating my toast,

I ordered another cup of tea and a plate of Gorgonzola, walnuts, and honey. I was vibrating a little from the lack of sleep. I was taking my time, though, allowing myself to savor the moment. I could be anyone I wanted to be.

A young woman and twin girls, probably around the age of five, sat down at the table next to me. They were dressed in several layers, and it took the young woman some time to get each layer off the children. First came the parkas, that one was easy. Next the two thick sweaters, over their heads, bringing loose blond hair up with static. Then, a long-sleeved shirt, one each. And there was more: one had a giant necklace of felt balls, the other a lip balm hanging on a fabric chain, and each in turn needed to be removed and filed away into the young woman's bag. But right after she opened her bag to do so, each little girl demanded her necklace back, and just as quickly as the woman had shoved them in her bag, she retrieved them again, handing each necklace back to its owner. Only she had mixed them up accidentally, disobeying the social order, and there was shrieking centering on a new conflict. One girl denied having the other's precious necklace, claiming it to be hers, and she was refusing to trade back. There was grabbing over the table settings and breaking up of the grabbing. The young woman was starting to seem embarrassed and looked around to see if anyone else in the café was watching. It was clear now that she was not, in fact, the little girls' mother. They were wielding a certain power over her, and her mannerisms seemed practiced but not intuitive, like those of someone trying to master something that didn't come naturally to her. An aunt, maybe. But no, on second thought, an aunt would be magical, the girls would see her not very often, they would acquiesce, they would behave to impress her. This was more than likely a caretaker, and she was probably new, because the girls didn't listen to her and there didn't seem to be a set code among them. She kept asking them to use inside voices, but the girls ramped up their whining with each of her pleadings. She begged them to trade back necklaces and they refused, flatly, and I saw a glint in one of the girls' eyes as if to say to her sister, "Let's keep fucking with her." Eventually one girl tipped over her water glass, and the woman scrambled to find a napkin to clean it up before it spilled over into their laps. The other child just sat there and didn't help.

I flagged the waitress, who was slammed. She brought them over a dishrag, and the woman began mopping up liquid, which had pooled onto the floor. The little girls swung their legs gleefully, until one foot caught the woman on her ear. That was it, she got out from under the table. They were leaving. They wouldn't get a treat after all, and she would be reporting all this to their mother at the end of the day. The girls started to cry, and as their despair escalated, the young woman began to look desperate. "Okay, fine," she said to them. "I won't tell her if you promise to behave." That shut them up. One of them negotiated: "Let us watch a video." This had become unbearable to witness. She was cornered, the young woman, by two little wolves. But she capitulated, and it was settled, the girls loosened and began to obey. The young woman put back on their layers of clothing, and handed both girls their mittens, which they put on independently, without help, all four thumbs in all four thumbholes. The waitress came back with my bill.

I left the café and sat for a while listening to a busker. As the city blew by me, I sank deeper into solitude. Asa would soon be picking the kids up from school. He would return home expecting me to be there, but the house would be empty and cold. Phin would be contemplative; Asa would have to redirect him, start a fire. Eden would cry out for me. They would race around the house, expecting me to pop out from behind a corner. They would ask Asa when I was coming back. He would change the subject.

But maybe they wouldn't miss me. Maybe they wouldn't even notice. Asa usually stopped at the country store on the rare occasions when he picked them up, something I never did, and who knows, maybe he'd let them watch more than one movie that night. They might be happy I was gone. They might say to him, over ice cream, "I hope she doesn't come back." Well, maybe I wouldn't. Then again it was possible they would notice how little butter Asa used in their noodles, and then they would want me again.

I checked my email again and saw there was still no response from Celeste. Why wasn't she writing me back? Had I done something to upset her? No—when I reread my email to her, I found it charming, and only partially a lie. Where was she now? After the fiber store she had stopped giving me information, and for all I knew, she was gone, driving in a car or boarding a train, on her way somewhere. It started to rain, soaking me almost instantly, and I ran into the first doorway I could find.

I was in a women's clothing store, expensive, with spare offerings. The walls were faded red brick, the ceiling white. Down the center of the room, which was lined with steel racks of billowing, expressionistic clothing, was a wooden table covered with neat rows of shoes. It was familiar in some ways, but more impressive, more important-feeling than any store I had ever entered. At the far end of the table was a case displaying tiny jars of face cream, white with black plastic caps. Next to the display case, on a wooden stool, sat an old steamer trunk filled with silk scarves.

I walked slowly around the room—there was no saleswoman I could see—letting myself admire each piece of clothing, flipping through the racks carefully as if I were looking for something in particular, imagining myself in situations where this glamour would be warranted. The beauty captivated me; I was saturated with longing, or maybe it was just appreciation that had over the years hardened into longing. I let my hands caress the fabrics. I thought of painting, I thought of the ocean, I was absorbed in the swirl of textile and color. It was cold and I wrapped my arms around my own soft sweater, sort of waltzing in slow motion, satisfied with my recent purchase and unable to imagine room for more. My eyes were closed. I had lost myself to anxiety and sleeplessness, and had wandered into my own dream. When I came to the end of a rack, I stopped at the jars of face cream.

The store was mostly empty. On the other side of the room, however, slightly obscured by the display case between us, was a woman with her back to me. She was listening intently to a saleswoman, each of them holding one of the containers of ointment. The saleswoman was describing the "Crème Reine," which was made by a little-known convent of nuns in the French countryside, and whose price tag reflected the care and secrecy of its creation. The nuns rose at three thirty each morning to begin mixing the lotion, breaking just a few times a day, to attend chapel and worship. The holy cream was blessed by each of them, and the concentration and commitment of their spiritual practice could undoubtedly be seen in the quality of the product; the jars had been flying off the shelves in over ten countries across the world, a shock to the company, which saw the line as an experiment in collaboration at best.

Although the woman listening had her back to me, I became overwhelmed by a feeling of familiarity. She was wearing a loose-fitting camel trench coat, which, while slightly too big, seemed purposeful and elegant. She had messy brown hair tinged with gold, tucked into her linen scarf, which was gray with a green floral pattern—the whole look uninterested in cohesion, as if she had been late to depart and had dressed in a rush, and was all the more captivating as a result. As she flipped her hair with her hand, I smelled tangerine and honey. I watched as she listened to the saleswoman's pitch for the Crème Reine, saw her long, browned thumbs curved back, her light blue nails gently stroking the side of the jar, her smooth nail bed, the soft edge of a green sweater visible at the coat's wrists. The sensation of beauty overpowered me. I wanted to be a part of it, to step inside her orbit. Without thinking, I reached for the display case and weighed a cold container of lotion against the palm of my hand too.

Suddenly, the woman turned and walked toward me. As she did, I woke up. Yes, the familiarity was warranted. Yes, I had seen those thumbs, those wrists, those weathered boots, that upturn of the cheekbone before; that face had been etched into the deepest bedrock of my consciousness. In that moment, I crouched down with the reflexes of a Neolithic cat, practically crawling to the dressing room twenty feet away. Celeste set down the cream in the display case—it was a tester—and picked up another for purchase. Had she seen me? She must have. She must have recognized me. I had been right in front of her. But then I realized that while I knew her so well, and while in some ways she knew me, the relationship was visually one-sided. I was safe.

I eased the door of the dressing room shut. Hadn't I come to New York for this very purpose? Hadn't I been tracking her? How, then, was it a surprise to actually find her? Wouldn't I, upon discovering her, experience a sense of satisfaction and relief? As I leaned against the door, breathing heavily, a part of me felt like introducing myself, explaining who I was. The other part felt like a sociopath.

And what would I say, anyway? What would *she* say? All at once, I felt defensive. I heard my argument in my head: I had been invited into her world, I didn't intrude. Yes, that was right—she had invited me in. She was the photographer, she was the subject, she was the object, she was the art, and so was her life. It wasn't my fault I was intricately familiar with her every move, so much so that I had found the two of us together in this store, almost by accident. She had asked for this, she had made it possible.

And then I realized that, if I knew her this intimately, surely I wasn't the only one. How many of us were there, the observers? How many of us were her friends? Did that number include me? Yes, I was the only one hiding in the dressing room today, but wasn't I more than just a voyeur? Remember, I told myself, I was a safe person. I was harmless. I knew her now, a little bit. I shared some of her secrets. I knew how badly she needed help, how she wanted to go back to work full-time but didn't have childcare. I knew what motherhood felt like, the suffocation. But what about the people watching her who were filled with rage? Wasn't she worried about what they were seeing, how they were interpreting her personal diary, the places she ate, the parks where she walked her dog? What were they holding in their trembling hands when they caught a whiff of her intoxicating odor? I became worried about her. I peeked through the crack in the door to see what she would do next.

Celeste had brought the Crème Reine to the register. At her feet was a stroller, and in it was her younger son, a little older than Eden. He was holding a waxed bakery bag in one fist and an enormous croissant in the other. He was whining. He didn't like his treat. Celeste put her card down and leaned over to speak with him. He continued to whine, and she whispered angrily at him to be quiet. But he wouldn't. "It's too crumbly," he wailed. "I don't want it." He threw the croissant on the floor of the shop. Celeste quickly retrieved it, and her whispering became louder, more ferocious. She furiously wrapped the croissant in the waxed bag, but as she did, she seemed to realize her vulnerability. She brightened for the saleswoman and laughed it off, what a darling. She brought up something else, different, to lighten the mood, and all was well again. Still, I was concerned about her. She was so stressed; it was obvious. Although Celeste tried to hide it, I could see that trapped feeling, that desire to work that was in deep conflict with the need to protect her children from a world without Mother. Maybe I could help—maybe I could reason with the boy, loosen him up a bit, just a stranger with a funny joke; I could pretend to want a bite of his yummy snack. These are the things mothers do for each other. I closed my eyes and took a deep breath. But by the time I came out of the dressing room, Celeste was gone.

I rushed outside. The rain had subsided but several umbrellas still obscured my view. There were puddles on the sidewalk. I dodged through the workday foot traffic.

Just when I thought I had lost her, I caught sight of Celeste again; she was standing at the mouth of the subway on the corner, and she was yelling. Her son was sobbing. She had unwrapped the croissant again and was waving it in front of his face. And as he attempted to swat it away, she threw it roughly in his lap. The boy tried to shove it back into the bakery bag, which was now ripping, but he couldn't fit it inside. Then he changed his mind, and instead of trying to put it away, he gave up and threw the croissant over the side of the stroller, where it landed in a deep puddle of city filth. The dirty water splashed onto Celeste's camel coat, and that was when she lost control. She picked up the sodden croissant and rammed it into the little boy's face. Then she leaned the stroller back and made her way into the subway, step by step, as he wept.

I followed the sobs underground. At the first landing on the stairs, I bumped into a man who was some sort of messenger, holding a stack of manila folders. He dropped the top third of the stack onto the wet concrete and the contents emptied, immediately becoming dirty and soaked. A few people trampled the folders in their haste to catch the next train. The man was moaning; he was obviously concerned about the state of his papers. But I was blinded by my mission. I cared about nothing else, there was no room for remorse or humility. To stop now would be to give up my one chance.

I continued in pursuit of Celeste, afraid of losing her in the crowd. I hopped two steps at a time to the bottom of the stairs, wet boots squeaking against concrete, and there was Celeste making her way through the service door toward the platform. I needed to see her up close again. I needed to confirm that it was really her. Because how could it have been? The Celeste I knew was patient, something I had never been. And she was gluten-free!

My desire to speak to her face-to-face was so deep, it was painful. There was a tightening in my chest. The loudspeaker announced the express train's imminent arrival. Celeste, I could see her, she was making her way up the platform with the stroller, and I managed to squeeze through the service door behind a tiny old woman pulling a cart of groceries. I was nearly there. I had lost feeling in my body. I was only intention and vapor and desire and will. Her son, I had to see him. I wanted to make him laugh. I raised my hand as if to motion Celeste to stop—maybe I even called out for her, yelling her name. I was sprinting, the floor was slick; it had become a matter of life and death. I was close enough now that if I reached out, I could touch Celeste's shoulder, and suddenly I flew forward as if pushed, colliding with her. I felt her hair against my face, a rush to my senses. There was a gust of hot wind from the approaching train, the mind-numbing screech of metal on metal, the taste in my mouth of what rats dream about. There was the pounding of my breast as Celeste and I met at last, and I felt the smooth fabric of her coat against my left cheek just before the cold cement. Someone screamed, and then—darkness.

Just the other day I had received a call from the town clerk requesting that I make a pie for this year's fall festival. She left a message explaining the concept: select people would bake desserts, and after a barbecue chicken supper at town hall, those desserts would be sold to raise money for the volunteer fire department. I complained about this later to Asa, who said I should refuse. He said to tell them I was a woman who did not make pies. He said they should have asked him instead, that we needed to create a culture of men baking. But there was a part of me, the part that had once tried to knit a child's hat, that wanted to be the kind of woman who shows up smelling of woodsmoke, wearing a hand-knit sweater, and holding the best pie. The pie everyone can't stop talking about. Perhaps, in this vision, the holes in my sweater would be from decades of fixing my own tractor, as opposed to the ones there now, from moths.

Making pies was something my mother never did and, by default, something I never learned how to do. On top of that, I didn't find pies delicious. A golden crust and warm fruit, while much beloved and discussed qualities in the Northeast, were details that repelled me. I preferred a good chocolate pudding. But I called the clerk back and agreed to make a berry buckle, a compromise I thought generous.

I had seen a recipe for a fruit buckle in a women's magazine at the dentist. I had ripped out the page then, and it was this crumpled paper, dug out of the recycling, that I turned to. My god, it was simple. I whisked together flour, milk, sugar, baking soda, and salt. I dropped a whole stick of butter on a cast-iron pan and shoved it into the preheating oven. In a separate bowl I put frozen blueberries we had picked earlier in summer, and some maple syrup, stirring absentmindedly while looking out the window. I poured the batter, which was already rising importantly, onto the melted butter in the pan, and spooned the blueberry mixture on top in haphazard lumps. I could get used to this, I thought. My children could get used to this, the smell of pie and the promise of that kind of childhood. I was undoing decades of my mother's neglect. I put the crumpled recipe on the fridge and secured it with a magnet. I smiled. I would fool them. I was fooling myself. Maybe now I was a real New Englander, with a secret recipe that had been handed down through generations.

I listened to the clerk's message again, and this time her demands were a comfort to me. There was safety in this simple fact—we lived here. Someone was expecting us to be somewhere, to do something. Even if these expectations were sometimes stifling, they also meant I wasn't completely alone. I had a vision of my children getting older, climbing down the school bus stairs, getting dropped off at the musty library. I pictured myself sledding down our long driveway to the town hall to vote, arriving red-faced, woolens caked in snow, filling in the little round bubbles to perfect black. I had an idea of myself that was starting to fill in too.

I made the buckle. And if they wanted me to, I'd make it every year. I'd make it every season. Maybe I'd use plums too. I'd combine fruits! I'd pick for storage with more purpose. I'd make sure the berries weren't so heavy that they'd burst through the batter. I thought about baskets, about which ones I'd bring to the pick-your-own, about the farms I'd visit. I imagined the hat I would wear.

I delivered the buckle that afternoon at two, right before the parade. My children were riding in a float; they were supposed to throw candies. I was waiting at the end of the line, I waved at them, I felt my skirt flying with the wind of the autumn afternoon, and I knew that I had done my duty, I had given the people what they wanted, and I was there, dependable as always. Phin was holding Eden on his lap with the help of an older child, and he gazed at me, his mother, he saw the familiar wrinkles around my eyes, he had scanned the small crowd for my face. I cheered. I scrambled for the candies. And then I followed the parade and met my children in the town center and helped lift them down from the wagon, and we went to the picnic.

———

I was lying faceup on the subway platform. A woman stood over me. She was wearing a shower cap. She held out her hand, helped me to my feet. She handed me the container of Crème Reine that I had taken from the store in my haste, but which had gone unnoticed. My phone lay beside me on the cement; the screen was badly cracked. Another woman close by urged me to see a doctor. I apologized, gathered myself, and got up. My hip was throbbing. I turned in a circle and looked for Celeste, for her son, but they were gone.

The air was still. It smelled of standing water and garbage, with hints of sweaty skin, metal, and old fast food. I steadied. I didn't see any emergency lights, there was no collective dismay. It was a scene that never changes: the yellowish haze, the peeling posters of TV shows and mass market best sellers, the people wearing headphones and staring into space, the skittering of rodent paws on the tracks, the dripping of putrid liquid, the other inexplicable wetnesses, the spit on the cement, the discarded newspaper, the empty coffee cup, the avoidance of eye contact, the music drifting over from the opposite platform. I tossed the Crème Reine in a trash can and climbed the stairs.

I made it to my car, which was parked a few blocks away. And as I drove, each stoplight turned green just as I approached it, all the way up the West Side Highway. I saw the buildings whirring past in gray, red cranes streaking through the fog. The air in the car was cold, so I put the heat on. At first, I drove in silence, but then I turned the radio on to classical. My mind was blank, for what felt like the first time, like a sheet of white paper. I had nothing to distract me; I was completely open. But eventually, the blankness began to fill in.

Seven

In the Great North Woods there lived an owl. Every evening she would soar over the moon-brightened forest and perform loop-the-loops, allowing herself the freedom of unadulterated flight. She would fly right through clouds that misted cool on her feathers, careening above the circumference of the earth. Early one morning, just before dawn, she came to rest on the branch of a large ponderosa pine, the dooryard of the hollow she called home. Her front door was rounded and painted blue, and hanging in the middle was a holiday wreath. She had forgotten her keys, or she couldn't find them. She searched among her feathers, in the tiny pocket of her plaid vest, and behind her ear tuft, where she usually kept the stub of a pencil, its end chewed. Her glasses were a cheery red, broken in the middle and fixed with duct tape.

Just then, from behind a bough, there peered a raccoon;

all the owl could see was the strike of her black mask under a canopy of pine needles and the tips of her blue rain boots. When she caught her friend's eye, the raccoon emerged dramatically, holding the missing keys just out of reach, then disappearing in a swish behind the branch, a tease. So began the chase, around the trunk of the tree in spirals, pecking, flapping, and hissing, up and up to the top, all the way until there was nothing but sky left to scale, and then, as a swimmer flips at the end of a lap, back down again. The girls were gasping for air and laughing, finally finishing in a tangle at the front door. The owl's glasses had broken again, but it didn't matter; they'd broken before, it was part of life. Anyway, she liked to tinker.

Inside the owl's hollow were her many inventions: a netted crook for catching small birds; a sword that lit up on account of phosphorescent lichen set in a plastic bulb; a Rube Goldberg machine that cracked robins' eggs, toasted bread, and delivered breakfast on a tray; and a go-kart built around an old tricycle that shot out wings in midair. The owl grabbed a bag of dried grasshoppers for a snack, and adjusted her scarf. The raccoon jumped inside the go-kart with a whoop and, pulling some goggles down over her eyes, pedaled the vehicle as fast as she could out the open door, down the branch, and, without hesitation, over the edge, where she lifted off. The owl was right behind her.

The two friends flew together, side by side, over wild valleys and vast lakes, farms dotted with cows, a mountaintop dusted with snow, grinning through their windswept fur and feathers and enjoying the thrill of the skies. There were flashes of green, the glint of sun on stone, gray scree on the peaks, meadows pulsing with wildflowers, bees cavorting with the wind, the smell of pine resin, a salmon jumping backward over a rocky creek, and a butterfly perched on a reed, pumping its wings without hurrying. Above the forest flocks of birds swirled past in darkened clouds broken by pockets of light, dancing in tandem with the music of the earth.

———

I arrived at the bottom of my driveway and turned up soundlessly through an inch of wet leaves. My car glided up the road, making a trail all its own, smooth and slow. I parked, closed my car door, and breathed in deep, both feet on the dirt under the glow of a half-moon.

I could see the house and the wasps' nest under the eaves, outside the bay window in the living room. I could see the faintest outline of the wooden red toy barn sitting inside on the window seat ledge. The flowers in the garden had withered with the first frosts, the droopy zinnias with their straw hats, the mound of silvery catmint, the potted geranium I had forgotten to bring inside, the dinner bell on the hook by the clematis, still wrapped around the trellis pole but deflowered, browned, and past. Under the covered porch was a scattering of shoes: Asa's sneakers, Phin's beloved cowboy boots that had split at the toe crease, Eden's little Mary Janes caked with mud, my lime-green garden clogs. Asa had bought more dog food; the bag was there on the porch, probably too heavy for him to bring inside if Eden was on his hip. There was the gargoyle angel on the outer wall of the house that a sculptor friend had given me, cast with wet cow manure and cured by her woodstove, odorless and brown, blending in with the cedar clapboards.

I turned the doorknob gently; it was late, everyone was asleep. I let myself in and was met with the odor of plaster and coats, woodsmoke and mildew. For a moment I recognized the singular smell of my family, of our essence, of our stuff, and with a sensation of deep familiarity there was also something new. And then, as quickly as it came, it faded. I slipped off my boots, put them away in their right place, felt sand through my socks on the entryway rug, and turned on the mudroom light so I could see.

Acknowledgments

The following books were directly referenced in this novel: *Des femmes dans la maison: Anatomie de la vie domestique* by Dominique Doan et al. (Éditions Fernand Nathan, 1981) and *The Berenstain Bears Lend a Helping Hand* by Stan and Jan Berenstain (Random House, 1998).

Thank you to all who read early drafts. And especially to those who offered valuable feedback and/or ongoing support: Sam Kelman, Katherine Leiner, Dylan Leiner, Martha Rich, Sandy Edmonds, Therese Mageau, Suzanne Opton, Andrew Lipton, Peter Kelman, Marie Gewirtz, Meighan Gale, Kimberly Kol, Camille Guthrie, Taylor Katz, Tracy Penfield, Comfort Halsey-Leckerling, Cally McDougall, Adra Raine, Nick During, Kareen Obydol-Alexandre, Daisy Holman, Claire Typaldos, Kate Maclean, Melinda Haas, Jan Sandman. Thank you to Jack Kruse, an early teacher who encouraged me. Thank you to my mother, my first mentor, and to my father, who left early but is still here. Also, to Miriam Rodriguez. Thank you to my children: Theo and Juniper.

Many thanks to my editor, Joey McGarvey, for her brilliance, and to Daniel Slager and the wonderful team at Milkweed. And to Jenni Ferrari-Adler, my incomparable agent.

Thank you to Leanne Shapton, and to the Vermont Arts Council.

Special thanks to Sheila Heti.

Suzanne Opton

MAKENNA GOODMAN is a writer and editor of both fiction and nonfiction, based in Vermont. This is her first novel.

milkweed
editions

Founded as a nonprofit organization in 1980, Milkweed
Editions is an independent publisher. Our mission is to
identify, nurture and publish transformative literature,
and build an engaged community around it.

milkweed.org

Interior design by Mary Austin Speaker
Text typeset in Baskerville

Baskerville is a transitional typeface designed
in mid-eighteenth-century England by John
Baskerville, a wealthy industrialist who began his
career as a teacher of calligraphy and a carver of
gravestones. His admirers include such luminaries
of the printing world as Pierre Simon Fournier,
Giambattista Bodoni, and Benjamin Franklin.